Love Lingered

The Love Series
Book #3

By:
Keta Kendric

Keta Kendric/Hot Pen Publishing, LLC
P.O. Box 55060
Virginia Beach, VA 23471

Cover by: Author King Ellie

Edited by: A. L. Barron

ISBN: 978-1-956650-19-8/Love Lingered

Contents

Synopsis:

Dayton: Love is an illusion and as easily forgotten as a song lyric. I didn't believe in something that could be so easily dismissed…until Atlas walked into my life, lingered in my heart, and redefined the meaning.

Atlas: Love was a torturous mistress who ripped me to shreds one time too many. Now, all I needed was enough time to meet, have fun, and disappear before the drama showed up. I believed I had it all figured out…until Dayton entered my life. However, I soon found out that love wasn't done tormenting me.

Warning: This is a multicultural contemporary romance that contains explicit language, explicit sexual content and is intended for adults.

Chapter One

Atlas

The high from my performance continued to course through me like pulses of electricity running through my veins. I almost didn't want to wash off the exhilarating mix of multiple female scents and perfumes. There was no better motivator or boost to my self-esteem than to have hundreds of women ready to fight each other just to see me.

The attention was next level, something for which I didn't have to beg. People paid to see me, to get a second of my attention. Many of the guys took it for granted—didn't appreciate what that level of attention did for their confidence, self-esteem, and even their mental health.

A silly smile rested on my lips at the memory of the woman who handed me her purse and told me to do what-ever I wanted with her finances. And the one who promised me she would come on the spot if I said her name. The way they had fought to be chosen to be on stage with me.

Who needed a fight club, aggressive sports arenas, or any other number of stress relievers when there was danc-ing?

"Shit!"

I jolted upright at the hard slap that struck my back like a thunderclap and yanked me out of my moment of reflective elation. Reflexively, my muscles clinched.

"Are you all right, old man? At your decrepit old age, you'll have to cut down on all that shaking and gyrating. If you shake something loose or off, I'm not picking it up," Ry teased while opening his locker three doors down from mine and tossing his gym bag inside.

I couldn't help a peal of boisterous laughter. The twins, Rylan and Raylen, always gave me shit about starting my dancing career so late in life. Their version of late in life was when I began working at the club three and a half years ago at twenty-seven. At thirty, I was in better shape than some of the guys in their early twenties.

Quiet Chaos was one of the few strip clubs in the area, and with its large size and classy accommodations, customers visited from miles around, some driving in from cities and states that neighbored Virginia. With the steady influx of customers, most of the dancers averaged five grand per night on the weekends. Not bad, considering this was my weekend job.

"For a moment, it looked like you weren't going to leave any money for the rest of us," Raylen said, walking up and grinning while rummaging around in the locker he shared with his brother. You rarely saw one without the other, even on stage.

I chuckled but didn't offer a reply. I would be taking home sixty-five hundred dollars after the house took their percentage.

I imagined *her,* the redhead who kept invading my thoughts. I had her to thank for the extra effort I poured into my performance tonight. Her hair wasn't fire-engine red but a unique honey-red color of lengthy, straight hair that framed her smooth baby face.

Her body was a prelude to a daydream. Shapely curves with a small waist that alluded to good genes or a robust exercise routine. She was dressed in a silky black halter-top romper that added a touch of class to how she presented her sexy body. However, it wasn't her clothing that drew my attention. It was everything else: her smile, her expressions, mannerisms, and her radiant light-honey skin tone. Her aura spread through the room, and people, men and women, gravitated to her like she was the center of her own universe.

In three and a half years of dancing, this was the first time my focus had narrowed down to a steady enough rhythm to pinpoint finite details about a woman. I didn't know the intriguing woman's name, but her presence, even with the roaring crowd, piqued my interest and kept a firm hold on it.

"I saw who you kept looking at, old man," Raylen teased. "She is feisty, too. I made a pass at her, and she told me to grow up about five more years before I even approached her. I promise I fell in love right there on the spot. I mean, look at me. If a woman can look at me half naked and tell me to get out of her face and not make it sound like an insult all at the same time...my man, she's straight fire."

"Whew!" Rylan shouted like he felt the exhilaration his brother was experiencing. I sensed both sets of their eyes narrowing in on me now.

"You were dancing just for her, weren't you?" Raylen asked, his expectant gaze pinned on mine.

I shrugged. "I don't know who you're talking about. We get out there and dance. Our job is to give the customers the best experiences we can, put smiles on faces, and get them hyped up," I lied.

I knew exactly who he was talking about. We were the entertainment under this roof, but *she* was very much *my* entertainment and had also caught the attention of these twins. They were rarely this vocal about a woman.

"When you go out there on your mingling tour later, you think you can get her to go home with you tonight?" Raylen asked, one of his brows hiked with curiosity, but I also heard the challenge in his question.

My plan after my shower *was* to go and see if I could find her, but now that she was on a few other radars, I wasn't so sure. After all, we were in the last place you went to meet someone. Maybe I should do some good old-fashioned legwork and go at this from another, more dignified angle. That way, she'd take my interest seriously.

Our short connection kept playing out in my head. She had been one of the women volunteering, reaching out for me to bring her up on stage, and I had gone to her. However, with a closer view of her, I saw more than I bargained for and changed my mind at the last moment. It was a first for me, a tiny spark in time that made an impact that sent lasting ripples through me. Did it mean something, or was I feasting on a figment of my imagination?

***

Two hours later.

My intention had been to pick up a willing woman and head to my penthouse apartment in downtown Richmond, but the motivation wasn't there anymore. However, there was one thing I did want to know.

Now, I hung out in the wide hallway that led to the restrooms. Several seating areas aligned the expanse of the hall to accommodate the women, like the one who just staggered into one of the chairs and snatched the heel off of her left foot.

As soon as the woman I was waiting for walked out of the bathroom, we made eye contact, and I smiled. I'd been pretending to be on my phone, the one thing keeping the other women off me long enough to snag the attention of this specific one. I'd seen her sharing a table with *the one* I couldn't get out of my head.

All it took was my smile, a slight head gesture, and me shoving my phone in my back pocket for her to slow her steps and turn in my direction. I reached out for her hand to solidify our connection. She was pretty but too skinny for my taste.

"Hey! I was waiting for him," one of the women waiting on the sidelines slurred. The one with me didn't even bother acknowledging the complainer at her back. I spun her, pretending to do a little dance from the music thumping into this hall before I pulled her into me like we were about to do the tango.

"You're sexy, but I only do threesomes. Are you down?"

"Hell...Yes!" she yelled, slurring and making the word yes, sound like a foreign language.

"I like the redhead you're sharing the table with. Would she be down for something like that?"

She nodded. "Yes, she might be down. I know I am. You want me to go and get her?"

"Yes, but first, what are your names?"

"I'm Katrina, and she's Dayton," she answered quickly.

"Katrina, I like to say full names when..." I lifted a brow so she could finish the sentence however her mind saw fit.

"Katrina Maxwell," she said breathlessly, understanding what I wanted. She was so tipsy, I doubted she noticed that I was keeping her steady on her feet.

"Katrina Maxwell," I whispered hotly in her ear, making her shiver when my lip scraped her lobe.

"What's Dayton's last name?"

"Her name is Dayton Davis, and we work together at Franklin Memorial Hospital."

The term loose-lips-sinks-ships came to mind. The additional information she'd given me about Dayton was a bonus. I nodded, clenching my bottom lip between my teeth.

The audience of about six women watching us from the sidelines wore expressions that indicated they wanted to do bodily harm to Katrina.

"Katrina Maxwell," I said to her. "Will you go and get your friend? I'll be right here waiting for you."

"All right. This has always been one of my fantasies," she said before dashing off on her mission. I considered myself a stand-up kind of guy, so I wasn't going to leave Katrina high and dry.

"Ry," I called, waving to rip his attention away from the five women surrounding him. He excused himself but, as expected, had trouble breaking away from the group.

When he finally made it to me, I gripped his shoulders, pulling him in for a talk.

"Did you see the woman I was with?" He nodded and peered at me with intrigue flashing in his gaze. Most of the guys believed that if I picked a woman, she was a diamond amongst cracked glass. I also made it my mission to help each of the guys with their problems, whether it be legal, financial, or other, so they respected me and my opinion. When I needed a favor like now, they didn't hesitate to help me.

"I just made Katrina a promise, and something else has come up. Would you make sure she's taken care of?"

He nodded hard. "Yes, you know I got your back," he said enthusiastically. He lifted his hand so I could reach up and slap palms with him.

"She said her fantasy was leaving here with one of us, so I need you to make sure she has the time of her life, but only her. No threesomes or anything." He nodded, his expressive eyes lifting, probably questioning why I was mentioning a threesome.

The last thing I wanted was him anywhere near Dayton.

"I got you," he promised.

"She's at table five. Make her feel extra special."

His smile widened, and an eager glimmer was set in his eyes before he marched away. I stroked a few hips and backs and even dished out a few friendly hugs before I entered the dim showroom and lingered in the darkest corner.

Ry was on his knees, kneeling in front of Katrina like he was professing his undying love. Her priceless smile lit up the room as she patted her chest like she couldn't take the sudden influx of attention. She'd forgotten all about me and my promises like I knew she would.

I stepped away, thinking of only one thing.

Dayton.

Chapter Two

Dayton

The clattering of spoons, forks, and knives against porcelain competed with the sound of smacking lips. The men in my life were pigs in more ways than one, and many of their bad habits had rubbed off on me. My take-no-prisoners attitude was aimed at them most times but was often carried out into the real world as well.

I'd been nicer to my family since they, my father's decision, had agreed to attend a few therapy sessions with me. On several occasions, I'd attempted to hash out our family issues but believed the issues ran deep enough to solicit professional insight.

"So, Day-day, what have you been up to? How are you living these days?" Delvin, the youngest of my three brothers, asked, calling me by the nickname they had given me since I was a toddler. Although he was the youngest boy, he still had two years on me at thirty-one.

"How do you think she is living? She has a pretty face and light skin. They treat her like a queen."

I aimed my fork at the oldest, Derrick. At thirty-six, he still lived with our father in the family home we were currently dining in. He saw nothing wrong with jabs like the one he just made about my skin tone, hence one of the reasons I believed we needed therapy.

"First of all. Don't answer for me. Second, I shouldn't have to remind you that I'm black. I receive substandard treatment like any other black person around people with bigoted views. Third, I'm a woman, so substandard treatment extends even further."

Twenty minutes in this house, and Derrick was already working my damn nerves and making me break my vow to be nicer.

"Why the hell did you start her off? I don't feel like spending this whole dinner being taught about women's rights and why women are ultimately smarter than men," Darryl, the middle boy, added with a tight grimace aimed in Derrick's direction.

"That attitude and you believing your dick is your lord and savior is why you will be on a fast train to hell," I added to piss him off.

My father, Douglas Davis, lifted a hand to stop this fight before it began. He'd been dealing with our antics for as long as I could remember. His wife, my mother, walked out and left my father for the man she'd been cheating on him with. At least, that was the rumor. I always sensed that there was more to that story. Unfortunately, we'd never know the details since my mother was killed by her lover months after leaving our father.

"Can we for once talk about something we can agree on, like high gas prices, or at least have fun arguing about sports? Even the weather is better than you lot talking about each other's body parts."

"I don't agree with this hot-ass weather. And if the weatherman keeps giving us the wrong forecast, I'm going to have to go down to that station and see what the problem is," Delvin stated while the rest of the table nodded.

I tuned them out. They all needed a class in gender sensitivity because my efforts since the day I could form words weren't working. Lord knows I'd tried to train these men but nothing I did would take. Their brains were infested with incurable diseases like egos, male pride, and misogyny.

"Day-day!"

I jumped.

"What? Why are you yelling?" I asked Darryl.

"Because everyone at this table was calling you?" he said. A glance around showed that all their eyes were aimed at me, revealing how far I had zoned out.

"What do you men want?" I asked, my face squinted in disgust.

"I was asking you how work is going and how that fine-ass friend of yours, Charlene, is doing?"

"Charlene doesn't want your broke ass," someone said under their breath, answering for me.

Darryl pursed his lips, ignoring the jab but kept his attention on me. "What man has your mind all twisted up inside your head?"

I aimed my fork in his direction with force.

"After surviving eighteen years in this house with you heathens, it's a wonder I have a brain. And do I look like the village idiot?" I didn't give any of them time to answer my question because they would have responded with a quick insult.

"I'm not fool enough to get myself hooked up with the likes of your species. You're only good for one thing, and, believe me, half the time, it's not even worth my time. I'm better off at home with my damn toys."

"Ewe! Girl, shut up that dirty rat trap you call a mouth. We aren't trying to hear all that mess. You have my damn chicken feeling like it's walking in my stomach," Darryl complained.

No subject was off-limits with us. We often put it all out there on the table for the rest of the crew to rip apart.

Sometimes, the only way to shut them the hell up was to say the vilest shit to come into my head.

"You can tell me about bending some chick named Candance over her desk, but you have a problem with my toys. Can you grow that slow-ass brain of yours up already?" I asked, catching a glimpse of Derrick's and Delvin's grossed-out faces.

My father put a stressed hand up to his forehead and squeezed. He'd heard and seen it all and then some.

"Nothing is worse than when that little demon's spawn was plugging her damn tampons up our asses, using us as her props so she'd know how to use them when the time came," Delvin blurted.

Our father, with his head still down, began shaking it in his palm while the rest of us were fighting to keep from laughing at some of the crazy shit I used to do to terrorize my brothers when we were younger.

All at once, the table erupted into laughter, and I could tell by the way my father's shoulders were shaking that he was laughing, too.

"How the hell else was I supposed to figure out how things worked? None of you knew how to use the things. Do you think I was crazy enough to test it out on myself first? Hell no!"

The laughter intensified. Darryl pointed at Delvin.

"He got it twice. We told him not to fall asleep in the living room, and he woke up with tampons sticking out of every hole she could find: ass, nose, mouth, and ears."

I bit into my lips, fighting hard not to laugh. We had our issues, but we always managed to laugh, at the expense of each other, but still laughing. I was only nine at the time of the famous tampon incidents. The fast little girls at school kept talking about tampons and getting their periods. I told my father that I was about to get my period, and he asked the lady at the pharmacy to pick me out some feminine products.

When I asked my father to show me how to use them, it was the first time I'd seen him struck dumb. He kept promising that he'd get one of his lady friends to show me, but when he took too long, I took matters into my own curious hands. I was jamming tampons into any hole they would fit into, including my brothers'.

"How the hell am I supposed to eat when we're sitting here talking about our sister shoving tampons up our asses?" Derrick asked.

"The same way you eat that hot tuna fish plate that your sugar momma, Thelma, got," Darryl teased Derrick.

My brothers were all handsome in their own way, but Derrick had always dated older women, some of them questionable.

"He's waiting for one of them old ass women to go on and kick the bucket so that he can collect on the insurance policy. You heard of the black widow? He's trying to be a widow, only in reverse. That's why the woman must be disabled or unstable for him to date her," Delvin added.

Unable to hold back, I laughed hard and long, loving that Derrick, with his want-to-be low-key messy ass, was getting teased. I was also glad the spotlight was off me.

This was a typical Sunday dinner for us. We didn't always get along, didn't always agree, and half the time, I wanted to punch one of them in the face, but we were family, and we loved and tolerated each other the best we knew how.

***

I waved at my father and Derrick across the room. They took their eyes off of watching some sports show long enough to wave back. My father didn't do hugs, so smiles and waves were about as far as he went with affection.

Delvin walked up to me and gave me a hug. He was the only man in this family who didn't find anything wrong with showing affection.

"Good seeing you, sis. Will you loan me about five hundred? Student loans haven't kicked in yet?"

He was studying to become a doctor while working full-time, so when he asked for a loan, it was often for a legitimate reason. And he always paid me back.

"I got you. I'll Cashapp you later."

"I appreciate it," he said, cupping my shoulder before walking back into the living room to take his seat.

I glanced back at the rest of my family, their faces aimed at the television. Right before I walked out, my gaze collided with my father's. He didn't smile or wave again but offered a single head nod that I returned before walking out the door.

Chapter Three

Atlas

A shower after a long, grueling workout was the next best thing to a professional massage. My friends and I retained our membership at one of the oldest gyms in the city because there was room to move around freely and relatively no wait time for equipment. I had a home gym, but the social aspects of attending one added value and a little extra flare to the workouts that I didn't get at home.

Ransome's expression, creased with pain, had me glancing at Trent and shaking my head. He had gone and gotten strung out on a woman. I had seen the woman who'd put that look on his face the night he stalked her at the club weeks ago. I couldn't blame him for wanting her, but he had to face reality. She met him at a club he was a stripper inside, and after their brief fling, she'd kicked him to the curb and decided to take her boyfriend back.

Maybe a story about one of my secret rendezvous would cheer him up. He and Trent always got a kick out of hearing about my latest conquest. Ever since my marriage got flushed down the toilet, I was reluctant to put much stock into building a relationship.

I was the oldest of the three of us, so it was my duty to keep the spirits of our group lifted.

"So," I began, dragging the word out to get their attention. "I spent last weekend with Bella Quinton, the model."

"I've heard of her," Trent stated, flashing me a proud gaze. "She's kind of young, isn't she?"

I shook my head.

"I met her at one of those charity events my family likes to attend so they can keep up the appearance of caring about helping people. Anyway," I sighed, "Our time ended up being a two-night event. The girl's a straight-up freak. Nothing like what you see in all of those innocent-looking pictures. She's twenty-five and says she lies about her age to book gigs. Her young appearance works to her advantage because many agencies in the industry want their models to look like girls wearing adult clothing."

That comment at least got Ransome to glance at me with a raised brow.

Trent nodded. He knew the industry because he often booked modeling gigs as well.

"She gets to keep some of the lingerie she models," I pointed out. "Even modeled some for me."

"No shit," Trent replied, but Ransome didn't.

Ransome was the hopeless romantic of our group, and right now, his misery was showing. It worried me to see him like this, knowing his happy-go-lucky spirit was broken.

Trent took over where I left off, retelling of one of his famous one-night stands. I was aware that he was only doing so as an attempt to cheer up Ransome.

"One of those famous one-night stands of yours is going to come back and bite you in the ass," I told Trent. "You tell women, *"It's only going to be one night"* and expect them to take the words to heart."

Trent narrowed his eyes at me before aiming a stiff finger in my direction.

"I can't believe you said that crap to me with a straight face. You tell women the same shit. Putting your fancy spin on it with a parting gift doesn't make it any less different."

"Touche," I replied with a chuckle. We had lost Ransome to whatever had taken over his mind despite our pitiful efforts to cheer him up. His gaze was fixed on his open locker.

I had to do something to cheer him up. Food was the next best thing.

***

An hour later.

Once we stepped into the restaurant and were seated, I told a bunch of corny-ass jokes that didn't get the reception I expected. Ransome was like the kid brother I never had and seeing him hurting made me hurt. Our bromance, as the guys at the club called it, had grown strong over the years.

Trent snapped his fingers in front of Ransome's face. "Earth to Ransome. Earth to Ransome. Ransome, you there?" This was the second time he'd been snapped out of a trance.

Trent quickly lost interest in Ransome. Instead, his attention was redirected, his gaze pinned, and his eyes squinting for a better view of someone.

"Aren't they your girlfriend's friends? Kind of hard to forget a group of women that damn fine," Trent asked Ransome, making me acknowledge the women to which he was referring. When my eyes landed on her, my heart seized in my chest, and when it restarted, it kicked back off with a thundering beat.

I waved stupidly when the ladies acknowledged us with smiles and waves of their own. Sitting next to Trent, I twisted and turned to get a better look at Dayton, the object of my desire. I was a man who had never fawned over a woman before, not even the one I had thought enough of to marry. However, Dayton had invaded my head space more than I cared to admit.

"Aren't you going to invite them to sit with us? Just because their friend dumped you, doesn't mean you need to blackball the rest of us," I told Ransome, whose whole demeanor shifted at the sight of the women.

"Hell no! Not so you two hounds can sink your teeth into them or play your little catch-and-release games," he replied.

Not with Dayton, I thought. I didn't even know the woman, but I already knew I'd do whatever it took to get her attention and hopefully more. Dayton made something within me come alive that I didn't even know had died. She invigorated my senses and livened up my spirit, even at a distance.

I cast a quick stank-eye at Ransome for his comment. He was hurting, so I'd let him get away with that one.

"Come on, man. They're hot. And not cheesy or slutty hot either. They're classy and hot, like that friend that dumped you. You have to admit, if you have to get dumped, it may as well be by a classy-ass hot chick like that," I said, teasing him.

My pettiness had slipped out, and I had gotten Ransome back a little for his quip about me and Trent's intentions.

I flashed Ransome pleading eyes, begging him to invite the ladies to our table. Instead, he picked up his plate and stood.

What was he doing?

"Excuse me, gentlemen," he said before he walked away, leaving Trent and me sitting there staring at his back.

"You ass," I hissed after him.

"Ladies, if you don't mind. May I please join you?" I heard him ask them.

Trent scooted out of our booth, too. Did he also intend to invite himself to the ladies' table?

I was already marching along with Trent toward their table before my brain fully processed my last thought. My eyes were clocking Dayton, her presence making an automatic smile surface.

"Mind if we join you, ladies?" I asked.

"Sure," Dayton answered with an inviting smile. I fought hard not to stare.

"I'm Dayton, and that's Callie," she introduced.

I made sure I beat Trent to Dayton's side of the booth which landed me in her personal space in the middle. I didn't care. She smelled like heaven, the vanilla and citrus scent closing my eyes as I fought not to inhale too deeply.

Cordial conversation kept us going, but the vibe at the table remained charged and tense in a disturbingly good way. I finally broke the silence by commenting on Callie's top, the one thing I could safely comment on without revealing what was truly drawing my attention.

Callie shared that she'd made the top herself and designed clothing for a living, which thankfully launched us into a conversation about fashion. I needed this distraction to tamp down the rapid beat of my pulse.

I tended to come on too strong and aggressive when I wanted something badly. It's what made me a good businessman and why my father didn't hesitate to put me in charge of our family business. I wanted Dayton, but I wasn't sure yet how to communicate it to her without being pushy.

"I need to get out of here. I have something to do. It was nice meeting you," Trent blurted, standing in a hurry before flashing a quick glance at Callie and over the table at Dayton.

Before I could get a word out, he stormed off. Knowing him the way that I did, something major was bothering him. Did it have something to do with one of the ladies at the table?

Although I was the one talking to Callie, I didn't miss the way she and Trent kept avoiding eye contact. Was it possible that her talking to me had pissed him off?

Trent wasn't the type to walk away, especially from a woman he'd taken an interest in.

Hmm.

Interesting.

However interesting my friend's peculiar behavior was, there was something much more exciting that had taken possession of my mind. She was about five-five, insanely sexy, and had me ready to set fire to my current dating status. All she had to do was say three words. *You're my man.*

Chapter Four

Dayton

Why did I get the sense that the man sitting next to me was watching my every move? He'd introduced himself as Atlas. Something about him reeled me in and made me fight to keep my eyes off him.

He'd parked himself right next to me in this tight booth and was sitting so close to me that I was sure we were breathing the same oxygen. His energy had me keyed into him enough that I forced myself to concentrate on everything except him.

Thankfully, he started talking to Callie about fashion. The smooth, sexy tone of his voice glided over his alluring lips and danced along my skin. Reluctantly, I dropped my gaze only for it to trace along the chiseled edge of his smooth jawline. Too slow to look away, he caught me watching him. His eyes clashed with mine for only a second—him letting me know that he was aware of the attention I was lavishing on him.

I reigned in my momentary lapse of control and redirected my energy. I believe with my whole heart and soul that cake makes everything better, so reaching down, I picked up my linen to unwrap my fork, only to have the fork slide from the napkin too fast.

The fork didn't clink to the table as I expected. It landed in the palm of Atlas's quick-moving hand. He didn't miss a beat in telling Callie what type of suit jacket cut he liked while handing me the fork without looking in my direction.

My eyes were all upside his head after his Captain-save-a-fork display. How the hell was he helping me and talking to Callie so casually, like there wasn't a whole other situation taking place at this table between him and me? I took the fork from his hand when he jiggled it to bring my attention to it.

The one called Trent hopped up, pulling all our attention. He gave a quick greeting and jetted out of there so fast it left us all staring at each other, asking an unspoken question.

What the hell is his problem?

Trent's departure freed up some space on my side of the table. Now it was just Mr. Fork Catcher and me on my side so he could finally relinquish the tight hold he had on my personal space. I was already leaning away from him, doing my best to avoid the weird energy wafting off him. My gaze went upside his head again.

"You can move over now," I said when there was a break in Ransome asking us about Charlene—again.

Atlas placed his left elbow on the table and propped his head up on his fist so that he could see me better. We were sitting so tightly in the booth; the move made this moment feel intimate.

"I don't want to move. I like being in your space."

"What?" I choked out, our conversation low since Ransome and Callie were busy chatting about something.

"I said..."

"I heard what you said, but why are you all up in my space?"

He shrugged. "It feels good. Comfortable. Warm and inviting."

I laughed.

"Um, first, I didn't invite you into my space. You invaded it. Second, I don't know you, and you don't know me, and even if I did know you, you wouldn't have been invited. Third, do you plan on scooting over any time today so that I can enjoy my cake in peace?"

With his elbow still on the table and his eyes still on mine, he moved over, putting about an inch between us. He may as well have not moved at all.

My eyes lifted and dropped, lifted and dropped, eyeballing him from his head to as far down as our tight seating arrangement allowed. He was a handsome man. Thick, light-brown, low-cropped hair, sexy, full lips, and crystal-like blue sparkling eyes that drew you in. He even had the nerve to have a dash of cute freckles, mostly gathered around his nose area. His scent was like fresh air rolling over a thick green forest.

I squinted, watching him watch me. What was his angle? I couldn't figure him out.

My fork was still in my hand, my cake untouched because he'd interrupted my peace.

"Who do you think you are, holding my space hostage?" I asked, unbending under his constant stare that flashed hints of intrigue and something more potent that I couldn't name.

"I'm only the man you're going to marry someday. That's all."

He spoke those words with such confidence that I couldn't help laughing, so loud this time it drew Ransome and Callie's attention.

They smiled at us, waiting for us to explain what I found so funny.

"It's nothing. My self-proclaimed future husband over here believes he has some right to invade my personal space."

Ransome and Callie's eyes bounced back and forth between us, but neither was willing to broach the subject.

"Are you staying? I'm going home," Callie announced, her eyes pinned on mine.

I nodded. "Yeah. I'm going to finish my cake and apparently petition to get my space back," I said, sending a quick glance at Atlas.

He still hadn't relinquished my personal space. The fact that I remembered his name was saying something. What? I didn't know yet.

"I'm going to cut out, too," Ransome said, standing. His update drew Atlas's attention.

"I'll walk. I need to stretch my legs," Ransome told Atlas, who must have been his ride.

"Are you sure?" Atlas asked. I didn't miss how Ransome's eyes flickered in my direction before he nodded at Atlas.

"Yeah. I could use the fresh air." Ransome gestured towards me and Callie. "It was nice seeing you again."

"You too."

"You as well," we returned before he turned and walked off. His bent posture, long face, and gloomy eyes spelled a broken heart. Charlene must have left one hell of an impression on that man. I believed he truly cared about her. I didn't think strippers got broken hearts, but what the hell did I know?

Callie reached across the table, placing her hand over mine. She didn't say anything, only gave me a look. My eyes bounced between her and Atlas, who was perfectly content, elbow still on the table, looking at me.

"I'll be fine. I'll call you later," I assured her.

After a long stare, she finally scooted out of the booth. She hadn't touched her coffee or the piece of cheesecake sitting in front of her. Callie leaving behind dessert was a clear indication that something was wrong.

My gaze chased her until my self-proclaimed future husband regained my attention. He still hadn't moved out of my space.

My phone buzzed before I could put him in his place. My elbow and forearm accidentally nudged him several times while I was pulling my phone out of my purse.

"Yes. Is everything okay?" I asked, doing my best not to let the concern racing through me show on my face. I turned away from Atlas, putting my back to him.

"How?" I questioned the voice on the other end of the line while turning further away from Atlas to keep him out of my business.

"I'm coming over. There's no way that information should be known."

I clicked off, and you know who was breathing down my neck. I turned, my shoulder brushing his chest.

"Okay. You're cute, and you've had your fun. I even forced myself to laugh, but now, you need to back the hell up out of my way. I've got things to do and people to see."

He lifted his hands in surrender before sliding out of the booth and standing when he caught the serious glint that must have been in my eyes. My gaze dropped to the small amount of space he'd left for me to squeeze past him on my way out.

The front of my body brushed across his torso before I turned and faced him. Our eyes locked and...*nothing and everything.*

The electricity in his blue eyes sparked, and the static in my deep brown ones sizzled while I searched his gaze, observing the charged connection being shared with just our eyes while our bodies remained immobile.

I noticed everything and not enough about him within seconds: the perfectly symmetrical angles of his jaw and the glowing texture of his lightly tanned skin.

He looked well put together, but a closer look allowed you to see the imperfections that created the full view of the magnificent canvas he created. The inch-long gash at the line of the left side of his chin. The little cut at the top corner of his lip that gave his smile a little extra twist to the right. A tiny patch of his right eyebrow was missing from another cut there.

The crease that formed between my eyes when I was processing something that puzzled me deepened the longer we stood in place staring at each other.

"I have to…"

"Can I …."

We said and stopped without continuing.

"You first," he said, our eyes still locked in this strange staring contest we were engaged in.

I aimed a thumb at the table. "Since you've volunteered yourself to be my husband, do your husbandly duties and pay for our lunch tab."

"Gladly," he replied before he leaned down, closing in on my face. I jerked back and placed a hand against his hard chest.

"How much do you value your face?" I questioned. His reply was a high-arching brow like he hadn't just been closing in for a kiss.

"If you put your lips any closer to my mouth, it's going to cost you a check with a lot of zeros to repair the damage I'm going to do to your face."

His lips twitched like he was fighting to keep from laughing. This man was seriously assuming I was playing with him.

"Too soon," he said, shrugging it off like his actions were no big deal. "Next time," he said, sounding sure before finally straightening to his usual height.

Next time, my ass. The man was nuts. He didn't know if I had all my screws but was willing to take his chances, I supposed.

I turned and stopped to glance back at him.

"You're strange. If I didn't have things to do, I'd give you a number for a good therapist you can see."

"Already have one," he replied, making me laugh. I shook my head in quiet amusement and took off before he could show me more of his crazy.

When I'd seen him dance a few weeks ago, his performance was one of the classier, sexy ones that had captured my full attention. Apparently, I was the one who captured his attention today, for a little while at least.

I took one last glance back, and he was still standing there smiling, and even had the nerve to wave. My footsteps quickened in case something in his mind snapped and made him come after me.

Chapter Five

Atlas

I believe I had done my best not to come on too strong with Dayton, but I believe I'd failed. Now, I was sure Dayton thought I was crazy. She had even threatened to rearrange my face for attempting to kiss her.

The idea that she could be serious about laying hands on me had turned some sick part of me on. Most women I interacted with followed my lead and fell for whatever charm I attempted to display.

Not Dayton. She wasn't the least bit affected by me. The notion made me like her that much more. As I already suspected, she would be a challenge. She would make me work for her attention. But I didn't mind it because it would make me appreciate her more.

I waved the waitress over to pay the bill, my body jittery in its attempt to contain the anxiousness oozing through my pores. I badly wanted to follow Dayton. From where I sat at the table, I had a view of the exit and a glimpse of the outside. However, I didn't know what she drove.

My leg jumped. My heart raced. I needed to pay the bill so I could leave.

As soon as the waitress walked up, I handed over my credit card, not caring about seeing the bill.

"If you're in a hurry, the bill is only forty-two dollars if you have cash."

I glanced up at the woman, finally noticing that she was barely out of her teens.

"Thank you. You're about to get a big tip. I do have cash," I said, shoving my credit card back into its slot in my wallet and pulling out the two hundred in cash I had inside. I handed it all over to her.

"Thank you, and enjoy the rest of your day," I called to the waitress, whose wide eyes and smile suggested she was pleased with her tip.

Now, it was time to see just how crazy Dayton could make me. She hadn't shown much interest in me per se. Still, her allowing me to invade her personal space and the way she smiled at my antics was enough to let me know she was at least intrigued.

Dayton was a spark of magic. She felt real and didn't strike me as the type of woman to play games. She would tell me what was on her mind.

The way I was initially drawn to her, the way I am now, rushing out of this restaurant just to get another glance at her. There was something about her that struck a chord with me, so much that I couldn't ignore the connection. I believe she'd felt it, too.

She was ready to rip me a new one when she stood, but there was a moment where we just existed in something magical. It was a connection I'd never even shared with my ex-wife, who I believed at the time that I loved and I was in love with. Therapy helped me acknowledge that I loved the idea of Holly and what she represented versus her as a person.

I stepped outside and dashed over to the valet stand. Fate was on my side today. Dayton was climbing into her black Acura. Thankfully, she was distracted by her phone and hadn't driven off yet. The stress on her face was almost palpable, the same stress I'd noticed earlier.

When she'd turned away from me at the table to take the call, I could feel the tension rolling off her. Something was going on, and although it wasn't my business, it didn't stop me from being concerned about her.

I had never contemplated doing something as weird and out of character as following a woman. Yet, here I was, anxiously awaiting my car so I could hop in and see where she was going. My leg jumped, and my head was on a constant swivel, one eye on her vanishing taillights, the other keeping an eye out for the valet.

Blessedly, he pulled up as she turned left about four blocks down.

The valet hopped out, and I hopped in. I almost took off, but I couldn't leave without giving the man some kind of tip. He'd walked away, heading toward his station at the edge of the driveway that fed into the street, probably thinking I was a cheap asshole. I reached into the center console and rummaged until I found the twenty I kept there and handed it over to him.

As soon as I merged into the intersection, I weaved through cars to reach the street in which Dayton had turned.

"Dammit," I muttered under my breath when I didn't see her. Maybe the traffic was heavy enough to slow her down. I'd have to make some aggressive moves to catch up like I was doing now, zipping in and out of traffic.

My neck stretched for a better view ahead of me. Was that her Acura eight, nine, or maybe even ten cars ahead of me? If that was her waiting at the same light as me, I could possibly make it through when it turned green.

The driver in front of me kept a constant eye on his rearview, likely concerned about why I was riding his ass. If only he knew what I was really doing?

"It is her," I muttered out loud. She made another left that would take her toward Morgan Boulevard and away from the city. The only things in that direction were low-budget hotels, a few businesses, and gas stations. The neighborhood itself wasn't in the safest part of town either.

I continued to trail her, not allowing myself to believe I was doing something creepy at all. She wouldn't spot me since she had never seen my car, but I still maintained three or four car lengths behind her.

Ten minutes of twists and turns later, and we were entering the not-so-safe part of Richmond, the Oak Grove area. Dayton turned into the parking lot of a Bigway Inn, a knockoff Holiday Inn-type hotel.

Disappointment socked me in the chest at the knowledge that she may be meeting someone at a seedy hotel. Why else would she be going to a hotel if not to meet another man?

This was a good example of why it wasn't a good idea to act on impulses. I had no business feeling jealous where this woman was concerned. I scanned the area as I crept through the near-empty parking lot. The hotel was an older one that needed a paint job and some construction. The freshly cut grass and well-maintained grounds kept it from falling into the rundown category.

I pulled in three cars down from where Dayton had parked in front of the two-story building with the outside walk-up stairs. She parked right where the edge of the stairs ended at her driver's side.

Who the hell is she meeting at this place?

Kids playing in the gated pool area to our right was all that livened up the place that would otherwise appear deserted despite the cars in the parking lot.

Dayton exited her car. Her pinched expression and the tension riding her body and bending her posture heightened my own stress level. Why would she deal with someone who had her that upset? I reasoned with myself that I wouldn't stress her out if she were my woman.

Instead of walking up the steps like I assumed she would, she walked past them and knocked on the door of the room located behind the path of the stairs. I leaned nearly into my passenger seat, stretched my neck, and strained my eyesight to see who would open the door.

Dammit.

Whoever opened the door remained out of my view. My grip on the steering wheel tightened, knowing she was inside a hotel room with someone. Rather than sit there looking stupid, I cranked my car. I was already being an idiot. There was no need to add stalker to my resume.

Another car came to a screeching stop beside the passenger side of mine. A big, burly African-American man slung his door open and hopped out. The sight of him made me keep my foot on the brake instead of backing out as I intended.

His blazing gaze shot in the direction of the room before he stalked around the front of his car. He headed toward the room Dayton had entered. The closer his steps drew him to the room, the more my heart rate hiked and pounded in my neck and temples.

He was standing in front of the hotel room's door now. With his hawking stance and his angry demeanor, he spelled trouble. And, dare I say it, he wasn't Dayton's type in the least bit. I didn't know her well, but I knew that much.

I cut my engine and rolled my front windows down to listen. Someone had opened the door for Dayton. Who was this angry man there to catch cheating, Dayton or the person who'd opened the door? This situation was getting stranger by the minute.

Was I truly about to watch Dayton get caught in the act of cheating? The man pounded on the door with the back of his fist like an angry ogre.

"Open this damn door, Loretta!" he yelled.

"Loretta?"

My head jerked back, and my face squinted into an even tighter knot at him calling for another woman.

What the hell was going on? Was Dayton cheating with some man's wife? I hadn't picked up on a lesbian vibe from her.

I slung my door open but didn't step out of the car right away because my wide eyes were stuck on the man, who was now kicking the door. Anger poured off him as he put his back and body into kicking the center of the door.

Other hotel guests cracked their doors open and pulled back their window curtains to witness the man yelling for Loretta to open up. I hopped out of my car. This was not my business, but I couldn't allow this man to hurt Dayton or Loretta.

Bam!

Bam!

Bam!

His hard kicks to the door sounded off like wicked drumbeats while the cheap door vibrated and threatened to come off the hinges from his hard licks.

The door gave and went flying open when the man sent another hard stomp to the center of it. He stormed in without warning. Although I couldn't understand the words he yelled, his thundering voice hyped up his violent actions.

I ran, unaware of what I was walking into, but determined to save Dayton. I stepped through the doorway, breathing hard and ready to fight if I had to, but...

What the hell?

"You ran up on the wrong one this time, you fucking woman-beating asshole," Dayton yelled at the man while striking him with some type of stick. The other woman, Loretta, was kicking and stomping him wherever her tennis shoe-covered feet landed.

The man swung wildly to stop the strikes coming at him, but Dayton was swinging what I believed was a baton so fast and accurately that his punches struck naked air.

I approached him from behind, gripped one of his tense shoulders, and swung him around. My fist connected with his jaw so hard that the punch vibrated up my arm, and he went down. Dayton cast me a quick glance, and her expression went from anger to recognition and then surprise before her gaze dropped to the man wobbling at my feet on the floor. All of those years of martial arts my parents forced me to attend had come in handy.

The man being on the floor half out of his mind wasn't good enough for Dayton because she went at him again, swinging the baton against his head, chest, stomach, and wherever it landed. Loretta followed Dayton's direction and began kicking the man in the groin and in the face. She stomped her tennis shoes into his man bits, her face so tense with anger, it told me that the man had hurt her mentally and physically.

The way they were beating this man concerned me. I didn't want them going to jail for manslaughter, which would happen if I didn't stop this. At this point the man only had the presence of mind to protect his face.

"Dayton, I believe he's had enough," I said in a placating tone.

She didn't stop her aggressive beat down, and neither did Loretta.

"Dayton. That's enough," I repeated.

Her head snapped up in my direction while she still swung the stick, not caring where it landed.

"Forever's not enough for this woman-beating asshole. He's been beating up on this woman for over five years."

Now, I understood their anger, but it didn't help me figure out who the woman was in relation to Dayton. After twenty or thirty more licks and kicks, they finally stopped.

The man could do no more than groan in pain at this point. He kept his hands over his face while his body did a lazy twist and turn motion in anticipation of more licks.

Winded, angry faces stared up at me. I prepared to back up, fearing they were going to start in on me just for being a man.

"Um. What's going on here?" I questioned, my eyes bouncing between Dayton and Loretta before dropping to the man.

"Ms. Loretta, go and pack your bags. Quickly. I have a feeling this asshole isn't going to be tracking you down and bothering you anymore."

The fact that Dayton addressed the woman as Ms. implied a level of respect and allowed me to see that the woman was at least forty. Ms. Loretta eyed me up and down and sent her scathing gaze down to the man before she turned and marched to the closet, snatching the light on before entering it.

When Ms. Loretta was out of sight, Dayton glanced casually down at the man to make sure he wasn't a threat before she stepped over him. The man flinched, lifting his hands to protect his face when she moved across him. She gripped me by the arm and tugged me closer to the front door.

"What the hell are you doing here? Did you follow me?" she asked, her sharp eyes telling me not to lie.

I considered lying but figured it was best to tell her the truth since she was the one holding a weapon. I didn't want to end up like the man still prone on the floor. I nodded.

"I did. I'm interested in you and…"

"And you decided the best way to get my attention was to follow me? Um, not normal and creepy as hell," she finished.

Her face remained in a tight grimace, her eyes scanning me up and down to determine if I was crazy or not.

"I know, and I apologize. It's been a long time since I've been interested in anyone, and I know it was wrong to follow you. Do I have any right to ask what's going on here?"

After a deep sigh and her eyes taking me in with a glint I couldn't identify, she glanced back before pointing a finger across her shoulder at the now groaning man.

"Ms. Loretta's a family friend. I found out that the asshole over there has been beating on her for years, and she's been hiding it. She's grown tired of his shit, and he won't let her move on with her life. I hid her here, but the asshole used the half-brain cell he has to track her phone. He called her and told her he was on his way to pick her up so he could bring her back home. All she wants is to move on since they aren't married. I didn't want things to get to this point, but I wasn't going to let him put his hands on her in front of me. Then, he broke into this room and thought it was a good idea to lift his hands to me. I did my best to break them."

The situation was serious, but I was so proud of her for standing up for herself and someone else. I couldn't help letting a smile slip.

"He got what he deserved. He deserves a lot more, but do you think he'll get the authorities involved? Will he retaliate later?" I asked.

She shot a quick glance over her shoulder at him, who was rocking in the fetal position, before returning her attention to me.

"Would you go around telling people that two women beat your ass? He would be a damn fool to come after me? I have three older brothers and a father who are all in great shape and don't mind packing heat. Messing with me is like stepping on a landmine. You lift a foot and try to move further and your ass becomes grass fertilizer. Right now, I'm doing that asshole a favor."

I wouldn't want to be the man on the receiving end of whatever the Davis family was dishing out. My gaze dropped to the obviously distressed man before Dayton reclaimed my attention.

"I know this isn't the most optimal time to ask this, but can I call you sometime?"

She bit into her bottom lip, thinking about my out of the blue question while glancing up at the ceiling. "I don't do relationships, but since you obviously have some crazy in you...I may consider...something."

She made the universal sign of the phone before reaching out a hand for mine, wiggling her fingers impatiently. I unlocked my phone and handed it to her. She talked while inputting what I hoped was her correct phone number.

"I'm not your girlfriend. I'm not your best friend. Hell, we aren't even friends. The best I can do at this point is to hook up with you to see if you'll be worth my time."

I fought a teasing smile. She didn't take any prisoners, that was for sure. I nodded.

"Okay. Hookups for now, but you have to at least give me a chance to change your mind."

She handed me my phone back.

"Whatever, stalker."

"I'm finished," Ms. Loretta called, interrupting the *talk* or whatever it was we were having. She dragged her suitcases behind her.

The man on the floor should have made me worry about approaching Dayton about anything, much less a relationship. However, this situation I'd invited myself into had a different impact on me. One, I was glad Dayton wasn't seeing anyone, and two, she wasn't the least bit afraid to stick up for herself. I was from a world where there were beasts as bad if not worse than the abusive man lying on that floor.

Dayton turned back to the man, casting an evil glance over him. He was facing the floor in an attempt to push up on his shaky knees.

"Let's go before I catch a charge," she told Ms. Loretta before turning and walking out. The woman followed her out of the broken door.

I followed, but not before casting one last glance at the man. The circumstances in which I had established a line of communication that got me Dayton's number weren't the best. Still, it put a big, silly smile on my face.

What a woman. Dayton would either put me in the hospital, affect my mental health, or make me a very happy man. For my sake and sanity, I prayed it would be option three.

Chapter Six

Dayton

I didn't know how I felt about Atlas following me. It was weird and, at the same time, flattering that he was into me that much. My only concern was if it was interest or mental instability. The last thing I needed in my life was some crazy-ass man stalking my every move, showing up at my job, and doing something that would get his ass locked up.

A smile brushed across my lips. I bet he thought I went to that hotel to meet up with some man, and if so, what the hell drove him to enter that room and punch that idiot in the face?

Was it that unpredictable side of him that drove me to give him my number? Did I enjoy that he had a hint of crazy that agreed with mine? Did I like that he'd handled a situation that would have terrified many into calling the cops?

He'd spoken calmly, suggesting that he believed the man had been beaten enough. The crazy thing was, I wasn't sure how far Ms. Loretta and I would have taken things if Atlas hadn't entered that room.

"You like it all," I mumbled to myself, fighting to keep a smile off my face. His hope for us to be more than fuck buddies was useless, but I admired his willingness to try. I wasn't a dateable woman. It was something I accepted about myself a long time ago.

I stopped attempting to form decent relationships with men in my early twenties. It was like beating my head against a brick wall. I wasn't emotionally mature or patient enough to be in a relationship and neither were the men I encountered.

Unlike most women who would keep trying despite their difficulties, I accepted my truth and didn't stress myself out over men. There was more than enough of them for me to have sex when I wanted it, dinner and drinks when I wanted it, and even a weekend getaway occasionally.

Right now, my mouth was too slick, my temper needed a leash, and ladylike tendencies avoided me like the plague.

"Hello," I answered my phone without checking the caller ID because I only received calls from Charlene, Callie, work, and scammers. I answered the scammers because I enjoyed talking shit to them.

"Hello, Dayton," the familiar male voice sounded, throwing me off guard since I expected to hear from my girls. Especially after avoiding their calls for the past few hours to make sure Ms. Loretta was settled.

"Hello?" It was a question.

"I know you can take care of yourself based on the way you had a man twice your size crying like a baby at your feet, but I had to know for my own peace of mind if you're okay?"

I didn't know how to feel about him calling me, especially not about him calling about my well-being.

"I'm fine. Ms. Loretta is safe and sound. The smile on her face was a gift. I haven't seen her smile in a very long time."

Why the hell was I telling him all this? I believe it was to stir the conversation away from me because I didn't know how to feel about him checking on me.

"You're a good person for standing up for her the way you did today. It's an admirable quality to possess."

"Thank you, but this is the fight I often fight on behalf of other women. I can't stand to see women being taken advantage of, unfairly treated, abused, or bullied. I'm hated for it often, but I'm loud about fighting for women in any capacity they need."

A long pause followed my statement. I was letting him know in a roundabout way that I wasn't the kind of woman to take shit from a man.

"I understand and respect what you do. I sometimes need reminding of how unfair this world can be to women. I'm not directly faced with the disadvantages and prejudices, so I often forget what's happening all around me. I'll admit I'm guilty of not fighting enough or even recognizing what doesn't affect me, but it doesn't mean I don't try to understand."

Was he saying what he thought I wanted to hear, or did he feel and believe the words he spoke? He sounded sincere, but people often spoke your language if it would benefit them. I would figure out if Atlas was a man of his word or if he was blowing smoke up my ass to get what he wanted. If all he wanted was sex, that was easy, a night or two, and he could move on. However, I got the impression that he would push me for more.

"Hello," he called. "Are you still there, Dayton?"

"I'm here," I finally answered. "I need to get going," I told him, although I was heading home to clean up and watch a few episodes of one of the three shows I was binge-watching.

"Okay, have a good night. Please call me anytime, day or night," he said.

My brows lifted. Like before, it sounded like he meant what he was saying.

"Good night," I said, hanging up and glancing at the phone like it would shed some insight on him. I couldn't figure him out, and it bothered me.

***

Atlas

Okay, so I followed her home? "It's not creepy," I muttered to myself. *I was concerned for her safety*, I kept saying to myself.

I was still telling myself this as I eased past her house a few minutes after she'd driven into her garage. Her upper-middle-class neighborhood and town-house style condo, even the Acura she drove, didn't fit her fiery personality.

Dayton was educated, had worked in healthcare administration for nearly a decade, had a good-paying job, and was willing to lay all she'd worked for on the line to help her friends, and now I was finding out, women in general.

I believed I already knew where she stood based on her only social media account. But, seeing her in action, fighting a man who could have seriously hurt her for another woman, spoke volumes. Everything in her life, even dating, was secondary to her fight to ensure she and other women were treated fairly and offered the same standards as men. Most men would have run the other way, but I was into Dayton more now than before. However, I worried about her. There must be a safer way to help others without putting her life in jeopardy.

How many other men had she struck down who could retaliate? How many enemies had she created? Some of us had fragile egos and made the worst kinds of enemies, sometimes just to save face.

At first, I wanted to follow Dayton because I couldn't satisfy my curiosity fast enough. Now, I was genuinely concerned for her safety. However, I had to think logically when it came to her. She wasn't the type of woman who wanted a savior, so I would have to help her only when she needed or asked for it.

Dayton was going to put me through my paces. The best I could do at this point was buckle up for the ride because I knew with a great degree of certainty that I wanted her in my life.

Chapter Seven

Atlas

The view from my twentieth-floor corner office was unusually calm. Cars moved, and people walked, talked, ate, and observed while ambling along the sidewalks, but it all played out like an old silent movie.

I hadn't received a text or call from Dayton and it had been three days, proof that she was being truthful about what she wanted from me. She would only call me when she wanted me in her bed.

The bitter pill was a tough one to swallow, but in dealing with a woman like Dayton, I kept reminding myself to check my ego at the door. As serious as I was about pursuing her, patience would go a long way to winning her over.

"Mr. Belair, you have a visitor. Ms. Sutton is here. She's not on the calendar but says you're expecting her."

The last person I wanted to see was the one my parents were shoving down my throat.

"Mr. Belair?" Kelly called when I took too long to answer. I could practically feel Evangeline Sutton's eyes rolling at my long pause through my assistant on the other end of the line. Despite what she thought, I didn't give a damn about what her parents or mine wanted.

"Thanks, Kelly. Give me ten minutes and send her in."

I met Kelly at Club Quiet Chaos three years ago. When I discovered her background and that she'd quit her last job for being passed over not once but twice for a position she was qualified for, I pulled her in as my assistant, making twice as much as the Human Resources job she'd walked away from. She turned out to be a blessing: hard-working, smart, and willing to learn new skills.

As the acting CEO of Belair Enterprises, I made tough decisions and did my best to be sympathetic to my employees' needs. The business started out as a small real estate company over thirty years ago and had grown into a multi-million-dollar company holding over two hundred timeshare hotel properties as well as other large real estate investments.

Kelly was the only person in the building who knew I danced at the club. Sometimes, I wore a mask while dancing and interacting with customers, and even when I didn't, no one had ever linked the dancer with the businessman. Some people turned to fight clubs and thrill-seeking to decompress and relieve stress. I danced.

After a short meditation session, I prepared to talk with the woman my family strongly wanted me to marry. They had been hoping for this union for three years, starting a few months after my divorce.

Evangeline's family had reached billionaire status. The achievement enticed my mother and father to press me harder to marry into the Sutton family as a way to up-grade us to that financial status. Offering me up to a woman I didn't love was of no consequence to them. As far as they were concerned, I was performing my duty as their son.

My parents' obsession with becoming billionaires was for nothing more than bragging rights. A title they could flex in front of their entitled friends. And they didn't give a damn about using me to get there.

I didn't make things any better because I'd enabled them by following through with some of the outrageous requests they'd asked me to do over the years. Therapy was helping me figure out if I was corrupted or had some kind of misguided loyalty to family. I was raised by two people who had questionable moral compasses. I was still sifting through years of compounded drama, one session at a time.

"You better fuck her and fuck her good enough to keep her interest because her father is prepared to sign a 100-million-dollar deal, and I don't want his daughter upset because you couldn't be bothered to entertain her properly. I get that you don't want to marry her, but I need you, son. Hire you a mistress to satisfy whatever needs she can't."

This was the speech my father had given me the last time the Sutton *billionaires* had flexed their money muscles. My mother had treated me to dinner later the same night and given me a similar speech after my father's face-to-face in this office.

My parents were planning to pimp me out to their billionaire friend's daughter, and I had been letting it happen. Now that Dayton was on my radar, the good sense I should have originally applied to this situation was finally kicking into gear.

"Atlas." Evangeline was calling my name before I even saw her face. It was her way of letting everyone in the beautifully decorated cubicles know that she was entering my office.

"Evangeline," I called, feigning enthusiasm that just wasn't there. As the heiress of her parents' billion-dollar real estate empire, Evangeline had never done an honest day of work in her life. She often shouted out her family business to her two million social media followers as a way of contributing to her family's empire, and they had named her some type of business ambassador to give the appearance that she had a legitimate job. I knew better. The woman made a career of attending social functions and showing off on social media.

I stood at Evangeline's approach, reminding myself to be the gentleman I was taught to be by some of the best etiquette tutors money could buy.

"Atlas," she whispered like I hadn't seen her at her family home two nights ago. The Suttons had invited the Belair's to their home for dinner. Her parents, along with mine, had confirmed what I suspected they were alluding to all along. They tossed around the word marriage so many times, I expected one or both sets of parents to whip out a ring and propose to Evangeline for me.

Now, she was throwing her arms around my neck in a tight embrace that I didn't initiate. Her blood-red lips pressed into my cheek.

"Mm," she said, not backing away. "You always smell so good."

For good measure, she placed another peck on my neck.

Evangeline was a good-looking woman, tall and lean, with an olive complexion compliments of the best spray tan expert in the city. She was always dressed to impress and the object of a lot of men's desire, but she didn't do it for me. There was no spark, no special fire roaring within me like when I was around Dayton.

I had been attracted to, had lusted after, had even had feelings for a few women, but the pull Dayton had on me was something I'd never experienced before.

When I dropped my hold, Evangeline backed away and thankfully walked around my desk to take one of the two chairs in front of it.

"I was in the neighborhood and decided to pay you a visit," she said.

My smile, although forced, enticed her smile to return.

"Thank you for checking on me," I told her. She hadn't called me in a few days, and my parents hadn't ordered me to issue myself out to her, so why had she shown up out of the blue? Was she doing her own legwork now?

Besides, I told my parents that I was dating someone so that they could pass the dick-issuing duties down to one of my cousins, who wouldn't mind it one bit.

"I'm going to get straight to the point," Evangeline stated, straightening in the chair. "I want you, and I will do whatever it takes to make us a household name," she blurted out.

I swallowed. Hard. My lack of a reply caused concern to play out in her waiting gaze before settling in the tense set of her shoulders.

"I'm seeing someone," I blurted

Her lips parted.

"I started seeing her this weekend."

"It can't be serious. You had me bent over that desk," she paused to point at my desk, "less than three weeks ago."

My gaze skated over to the area she'd been face-planted an hour after one of my father's visits. Evangeline hadn't given me much room to tell her no, either. It was like she, my parents, and her parents were all communicating, plotting to take me off the market by any means necessary.

"I wasn't seeing anyone when we hooked up," I pointed out to her.

She jerked her head back and hit me with a wicked side-eye.

"Is that what we did? Hooked up? Like I'm something that you can toss to the side when I'm no longer of interest? Some fleeting fling?"

She *was* a fleeting fling, but I was smart enough not to say that. I had to word this in a diplomatic way to protect her ego. If she went crying to her father, it could damage the long-standing and lucrative working relationship my parents had with hers.

"No, I didn't see you as just another hookup, and I hope I didn't sound disrespectful towards you. However, you have to admit that we never established that we were doing anything other than having sex. I wasn't obligated to commit myself to you, so I was free to seek out someone else. I would like to see where my new relationship could go."

She sat staring, her blinking eyes the only way I knew she had life still flowing through her veins. I saw her thinking up fancy words she could use on me to impose her will for the relationship she wanted despite what I'd just told her.

"We didn't establish what we were. No labels were applied, but if you just started seeing this other woman, you two couldn't have established anything solid either."

She wanted me to read between the lines and reach the conclusion she was implying. I would do no such thing. I would play the dummy that she assumed I must have been because there was no way in hell I was giving up my chance with Dayton to be with her. It didn't matter how much money her father was willing to invest. It was my parents' dream to become billionaires, not mine. It was their goals and egos at risk, not mine. They could date this woman for all I cared. I had already been through a marriage that they had initiated, and it turned out to be one of the biggest mistakes of my life.

On their behalf, I had worked my ass off and went way beyond a son's duties to earn my place in my family. This time, I was not willing to sacrifice my happiness to play the part they were assigning me.

"Atlas? Where did you go? You were zoned out," Evangeline stated, dragging me out of my head.

My phone buzzed, saving me from having to answer her.

"Mr. Belair, your ten-thirty is here," Kelly's voice called out.

"Thank you, Kelly. I'll be out in a few to greet them," I told her, knowing I didn't have a ten-thirty appointment. Kelly was getting a generous bonus. She paid attention to details better than anyone I knew and had rescued me from more than a few sharks that had swam into my office. This world was brutal, and one of the reasons why I was using dancing as a means of therapy.

I stood. Evangeline didn't. She glanced up at me under her lashes, clearly not ready for our conversation—her conversation—to end.

She finally stood and followed when I didn't give her a choice and walked around my desk toward my door. I waited at the door with the friendliest fake smile I could muster. She smiled, but I sensed the agitation she desperately fought to hide.

"I'll call you later," she said before strutting pass the cubicles to the main exit. She was petty enough to stir up trouble. I knew this world. Knew how vicious the people in it could be and, therefore, planned to keep a sharp eye on Evangeline.

Chapter Eight

Atlas

The crowd was already starting to filter into the club, their energy giving the place a pulse, although the music wasn't as loud, and the alcohol hadn't fully done its job yet. After our grueling rehearsal session ended thirty minutes ago, I'd relaxed under a long, hot shower.

Now, we were preparing for our performances.

"So, Trent, what's been up with you lately? You've been acting...off," I pointed out.

No answer. Only a blank stare like he wasn't aware I was even talking to him. Ransome lifted a curious eyebrow at me on behalf of Trent.

I made another attempt to initiate conversation but got nothing. What was up with him lately? He had been like this ever since we sat at that table with Charlene's friends.

"Trent!"

"Trent!"

He jumped, blinking out of a trance.

"Yeah. Why the heck are you yelling?"

"Because I've been calling your ass for a straight minute. What the hell is wrong with you?"

After a glance at Ransome and a head gesture toward Trent, I decided to rephrase the question.

"Should we be asking *who* is wrong with you instead?" I asked. Could both my friends be *woman*-sick? Was I reading too much into the way Trent was acting?

"I'm fine. Can't a man think?" he replied, sounding withdrawn, like he still wasn't fully in this locker room with us.

Others walked around, changed clothes, and some even practiced last-minute dance moves, but Ransome, Trent, and I shared our own little corner. We needed to have a therapy session.

I rambled on with Ransome's help until we pulled Trent into the here and now. However, it was his latest update that blew my hair back. I took a seat next to him on the bench and lowered my head to his level. Trent had been acting funny lately, and now I finally knew why.

"Dude, you look so serious right now. What are you saying? What do you mean, it's the same woman?" Ransome asked.

"Charlene's friend, Callie. I met her a year ago when I did that modeling gig in New York. She was the designer on set. We agreed to a brief fling and stuck to the agreement. But I never stopped thinking about her. Never stopped thinking that I might have made a mistake walking away from her."

Was this Trent, or had his brain been replaced with some type of new alien technology that no one knew about yet? Ransome drew closer, his wide eyes searching Trent's for understanding.

"The woman who had you all lovesick last year was Charlene's friend, Callie?" Ransome asked him while I assessed him closely. He was serious. He nodded and pointed at Ransome.

"That day in the restaurant when we joined you at their table, imagine my surprise when I sat in front of the one woman I actually liked. The one I wanted more time with. The one I never stopped thinking about. Somehow, the planets aligned and put us back in each other's paths. I can't make the same mistake I made the first time."

I had never heard Trent talk like this. It was like meeting a new man—one who was hiding a big chunk of himself from us. I waved a hand in front of his face.

"It looks like Trent, even sounds like him, but alien tech is generations ahead of ours," I said, giving him another quick once over.

"You two are looking at me like I've been abusing small animals all my life or some shit," Trent said, defending himself. He had to know how much difficulty we would have in believing he, who may have coined the term one-night stand, would be this distracted by a woman.

"Charlene's friend?" Ransome asked again, his expression one of open-mouthed disbelief.

"Yes, Charlene's friend, Callie." He aimed a stiff finger in my direction. "I'm not a fucking alien. I'm me. I can be more than a man-whore-prick. Cordial, polite, accommodating. Those are a few of the words the women I've dated have associated with me."

As much as it was unbelievable, I had to accept that we were all finally growing up. I couldn't sit there questioning Trent's motives for wanting Callie when I was as good as head over heels for Dayton already.

What was the likelihood that the three of us, who a year ago were swearing off women, would find connections with three women who showed up out of nowhere one night and pulled the rug out from under our feet?

***

Usually, after a dance night, my adrenaline flowed, and I replayed the night over in my head. Tonight, all that filled my head was Dayton. I wanted to see her. Wanted to leave this club and drive to her house.

"I fucking just got robbed!"

My head snapped up fast. Trent stormed into the locker room, his erratic breathing a clear indication that he wasn't pulling a prank.

"What? What happened?"

He sucked in a deep breath and blew it out.

"In the parking lot. Someone tried to run me over, and when I dropped my duffle bag, they scooped it up and took off. I didn't even get a license plate. Can't call the fucking cops because they hate us."

"Damn, man. I'm sorry. Are you okay?" I asked, walking up to him and placing an arm over his shoulder.

"I'm good. Nothing but my fucking ego is bruised. And I can't help thinking that Callie's ex is behind this shit."

"Wait, what?"

Ransome walked up, fresh from the shower, with a towel wrapped around his waist.

"I heard. Are you okay?" he asked Trent, walking up to him to get a good look in his eyes. "You think it's Callie's ex? The same Callie you just told us about today?

Trent nodded.

"What I didn't tell you was that I attended her fashion event and saw her ex-boyfriend there, following her around like a sick puppy. Later that night, the fucker spiked her drink, drugged her, and tried to take her home. I shut that shit down. Took her home with me. She went to the police station and filed a report the next day."

This was a lot of shit to swallow.

"And you've been keeping all this shit from us? How long ago did all of this go down?"

"Last week," he muttered.

Ransome released a deep sigh at the news while I hit Trent with a devastating side-eye.

"First, a sick fuck drugs your woman and tries to drag her off to God knows where to do God knows what. Then, you stopped a crime in the making, and you didn't think to tell us what the hell was going on?" I snapped my fingers in front of Trent's dazed eyes. He dragged his eyes up to meet my expectant gaze. "We want the full story, not some watered-down version," I told him.

He nodded, still dazed over what had just happened to him. I had a feeling that before all was said and done, one of us may end up in jail.

Chapter Nine

Atlas

"Atlas," Dayton answered my call on the fourth ring. This was my third try at calling her.

"Dayton. It's nice to hear your voice," I told her, not sure what to say now that she'd finally answered her phone.

"Do you even remember what my voice sounds like?" she asked, challenging my claim of missing her voice.

"Of course, I remember the sound of your voice. When you're not telling me I'm crazy or in your way, your voice sounds like something straight out of heaven.

"Well, then. You must have taken flattery 101. If you keep talking like that, I might put you on my first-to-call list."

"First-to-call list? What's that?"

"What does it sound like?" She answered my question with one of her own.

"It sounds like a list of men you call when you feel like you want to be bothered," I told her. The idea of such a list shoved another dagger into my heart where Dayton and our lack of an established relationship were concerned.

"That, Mr. Belair, is a better, more politically correct definition than the one that I have for it. I simply say it's my fuck buddy list."

I didn't like those words coming out of her mouth, especially in reference to me.

"I'm going to make it my mission to obliterate that dreaded list. By the time I'm done making you love me, you won't even be able to think those words, let alone say them."

Silence.

I believe I'd scared her.

Good.

"You sound so convincing. I don't know if I should be afraid that you're crazier than I think or terrified that you will somehow find a way to make it happen," she finally replied.

"Be terrified," I told her. I didn't know how I would win this tough-as-nails woman over, but there was something about her push against my plans for establishing us that kept pulling me in deeper.

"Okay. I'm shaking in my boots," she teased.

"What are you doing right now?"

I questioned her before she came up with an excuse to get off the phone.

"I'm driving to work. You?" she asked.

Interest. It was a one word question, but I didn't care. There may be hope for us after all.

"I'm already at work," I told her.

"You are? Doing what? Practicing your dance moves?"

I chuckled. "Dancing is not my only job. Personally, I use it as therapy."

"Therapy? You take your clothes off for strange women as some twisted form of therapy? It sounds like you need therapy for using *that* as therapy."

I laughed.

"My job outside the club is stressful, as is my family. Dancing relieves my stress, much like working out or taking a kickboxing class, and the bonus is I get paid to do it."

"I think I understand, but what do you do that makes your work life so stressful?" she questioned, sounding genuinely interested.

"I run my family's real estate company. Belair Enterprises. Have you heard of it?" I questioned, knowing that there weren't many in our area who hadn't heard of it.

"You run what? You're kidding, right?" she questioned, her tone hushed like others were listening in on our conversation.

"No. I'm not kidding. Dancing keeps me from having a nervous breakdown."

"Okay, now I get it. But. How are you going to find the time to convince me to forget about the title of *fuck buddies*?"

I chuckled. She was paying attention to what we were discussing, something I appreciated.

"I had to learn the hard way how to delegate duties, and once I did, I relieved myself of half my workload. If I need to get that percentage down to clear those words out of your head, then so be it."

"At least you know what's important," she responded.

"Of course, I know what's important. With that being said, when are you available to have dinner? I'll make it for you, or we can go to a restaurant of your choice."

An exaggerated pause made the silence sound as loud as a blaring siren.

"Um…" she dragged out. "I don't go out. I take it that you've never had a fuck buddy before?"

There goes that damn word again.

"No. I've never had a fuck buddy and don't plan on having one. And you have to play fair, Dayton. How can

I make you forget about that awful list if you won't even consider giving me a chance to present my case?"

"Not my problem," she said, unwilling to give me any leeway.

"How about we place a bet?"

"I'm listening," she replied.

"We go out. And if I can get you to admit that you had a good time by the end of the night, you go out with me again. If I fail, which I won't, you get to continue to call me by that expression I don't like, and I'll have to figure out another way to make you forget it."

"That sounds fair. I accept your bet," she said, making my brows shoot up with how quickly she replied.

"Are you free Friday, Saturday, or Sunday? You'll need at least four hours starting at 5 p.m.

"Let's go for Saturday. I have Sunday dinners with my family, and as much as they get on my nerves, I make time for them," she said, another unexpected revelation. Making time for family meant she wasn't selfish with her time, although I already knew that based on her actions in defending Ms. Loretta.

"You didn't ask where we were going," I told her.

"I don't think I want to know. I'd rather it be a surprise."

My smile morphed into a full-on grin. A woman who liked surprises. We were going to have a blast. Henry from the accounting department slowed his steps while walking past my office, no doubt wanting to know what was making me grin so openly.

"Maybe you can invite me to dinner with you on Sunday so I can meet your family," I told her teasingly.

"If you were an asshole, I *would* bring you to dinner with me, just to see my brothers and father rip you to shreds, but you've been acting right so far, so I won't feed you to the wolves just yet," she said.

She at least cared enough to protect me, although I knew she wasn't ready for me to go anywhere near her family.

"I've arrived at my destination. I'll talk to you later," she announced and I could hear her moving around inside her car.

"I'll talk to you this evening after you've showered, eaten dinner, and prepared yourself for us to have a long and very interesting conversation."

Her low chuckle sounded before she hung up.

The stupid smile on my face deepened, and the invisible ropes Dayton had lassoed around me tightened.

***

Dayton

Hanging with my girls for drinks was one of my favorite pastimes. Gossiping about our co-workers and talking about men like they were depraved animals made me feel better, even if most of it was bullshit. Reminiscing about the good old days was like a pill we popped that reset our moods and attitudes to power through the following week. It was all therapy, as far as I was concerned.

However, the words currently spilling out of Callie's mouth had me looking at her like she had replaced her brains with marbles. *Sneaking around. A secret boyfriend.* And to top it all off, her shady ass ex was their potential stalker. Frozen and staring, nothing moved but my occasionally blinking eyes.

"Say what now?" I asked, cupping my ear for dramatic effect after Callie's announcement that she'd attempted to cast off as casual conversation.

"You've been sneaking and freaking around with a stripper too?" I sucked in a deep breath. I needed to say this one word from my diaphragm.

"Dayem!"

My gaze bounced back and forth between the two women I believed I knew best. Callie had been keeping secrets, and it bugged the hell out of me that I hadn't been paying enough attention to figure out that something was up with her.

The biggest tell was her erratic behavior in that restaurant that day. She never got that chatty with people she didn't know. Plus, the way she and Trent did everything in their power to avoid each other. Were we dealing with a group of magical strippers or something?

"That super freak shit they do on stage must follow them home," I muttered under my breath. "They got my girls. They got my damn girls," I mumbled, continuing my low outburst, knowing full well they heard me ranting unnecessarily.

"All of the updates she just revealed to us about her and Trent possibly being stalked by her ex, and that's all you take from the story?" Charlene asked while leveling me with a chastising glare.

"Let me process this situation the way I want to, please. This one—" I turned in Callie's direction and stared her up and down with my nose scrunched up like she stunk.

"This one has been sneaking around with a stripper for over a year and is just now telling us. Oh, and let's not forget, hanging out with her dumb ass ex-boyfriend, whom I recall telling her, gave off psycho vibes when she was dating him. The motherfucker growled at me that time at the club for calling him out for watching our girl like she was a fucking raw steak and he the ravenous wolf."

My tone shifted quickly when I noticed sadness resting in Callie's droopy eyes.

"I can't believe he drugged you. What if Trent hadn't been there?" Charlene asked, stress lines visible on her forehead.

"I don't know what would have happened," she said, shrugging and letting her shoulders drop fast. "I assumed Donni understood that we were friends. We even talked on the phone every once in a while, and he never gave the impression that he wanted anything other than a friendship."

I hated to see Callie going through this kind of drama that I usually did my best to help women avoid or escape. How could I not notice that something was wrong with my own best friend?

I was usually the one who paid attention because I was like the big sister of the group. It wasn't because I was preoccupied with my own stripper. I'd seen Atlas once, and he was punching a guy in the face for me. I'd also agreed to go out with him, but it wasn't like I was pursuing a relationship with him.

Veering off course, I reminded myself.

"I take it he didn't want to take a chance of not being with you sexually, so he decided to drug you. That's some serious shit. Devious. It speaks for his warped mental state. He could have taken you someplace and raped you. And if he's a real sicko like I believe he is, he could have locked you up in a basement prison, or some shit crazy people like him do," I said, hemorrhaging my thoughts.

We continued for hours. Charlene and I offered encouragement and feedback to Callie while allowing her a safe space to talk about her feelings toward her ex and her developing relationship with Trent.

I received some serious side-eye action from them both when I mouthed off ways and methods of sending Callie's ex to jail since the police weren't doing their jobs. Seeing Callie's occasional smile despite the drama surrounding her life was the highlight of my evening.

Chapter Ten

Dayton

Now that the time had arrived, I wasn't sure if I wanted to go through with this date anymore. I didn't date. Back in the day, when I was all bright-eyed and bushy-tailed over dates, I got dumped or cheated on so many times I accepted that investing in a commitment wasn't for me. I wasn't willing to be fake and pretend that things were going well if they weren't. I was too honest, too opinionated.

Atlas possessed a determination that I appreciated. He wasn't a pushover and certainly wasn't afraid to go after what he wanted. Those were some of the reasons I'd agreed to this *date*, despite the bet we'd made.

Jeans and tennis shoes or something casual and comfortable were how he'd instructed me to dress tonight. He better not have me hiking in the woods because I wouldn't have a problem telling him what he can do with his trees and bugs.

He'd insisted on picking me up from my house. I proceeded to warn him that I owned a gun if he got the desire to peek into one of my windows.

The comment got a good laugh out of him despite me being kind of serious about it since he had followed me once before. That incident was a reminder for me to look out for any other signs that would help me determine if he was a stalker, mentally unstable, or worse. Hopefully, he was just confident and genuinely concerned. Those were qualities I could abide by.

My phone chirped. Atlas was outside. The knowledge sent a spark of unexpected excitement racing through me. My interest remained piqued while ideas of where he planned to take me started popping into my head. I shut off all my lights except a lamp in the living room, snatched up my purse, and opened the front door.

"Atlas," I called out, not used to seeing a man at my door, much less a tall, sexy, well-built one. I glanced around him to make sure we weren't being watched. The last thing I wanted was my nosey-ass neighbors gossiping about who was visiting my house. I lived in a quiet village of condos and townhouses, and although I enjoyed privacy in and around my property, stepping outside into the public view became open season for gossip and speculation.

"Dayton, my one and only," he called out, greeting me like I was his wife returning from a month-long trip. I offered him a polite smile before turning away to lock my door. The smile on my face said more than I cared to admit. I liked him, and that was saying something. Usually, it was lust and desire that temporarily drew me to a man. Atlas was likable.

"So, no greeting me with a kiss, a hug—nothing?" he asked while my back was to him.

"We are not on that level yet," I told him while completing the task of locking my door.

"Okay," he replied. The teasing glint in his eyes when I turned back to him said he didn't care about my rules.

He walked beside me during the short walk along my driveway until we reached his car, and then he opened my door and offered me a hand to climb inside. This action won him a few brownie points as most of the men who were interested in me didn't know the definition of chivalry, much less offered up some on my behalf.

"Thank you," I said graciously after taking his hand and sliding into the car.

"You're welcome," he replied before closing my door. I sniffed in the new car scent and glanced around the interior. It was an expensive-looking Mercedes that reflected his dual personality as a corporate businessman and stripper. I would venture to say his alter ego as a dancer was the one he preferred.

He marched around the car with quick strides, hopped in, and eased it to a quick start. The engine purred like a kitten as we eased back and out of my driveway.

"How do you keep your jobs and personalities separated? They're on opposite ends of the spectrum."

"I could ask you the same thing. Being a health care professional by day and a vigilante by night sounds like it would be difficult to maintain."

"Touché." I laughed.

"To answer your question, it is because the two jobs are so different that I'm able to separate the two. One, I have to do, and the other, I choose to do. One makes me feel like a puppet going through the motions to impress people I care nothing about. I tell myself I'm doing it for my family, but I can't honestly say why I continue doing it."

He sounded conflicted, like he was doing the stressful job to appease his family.

"So, if you figure it all out in your head and decide that being a CEO is not for you, you'll quit your job and become a full-time stripper?"

He scratched his head. "Putting it that way makes it sound like a decision that wouldn't be easily made. However, I wouldn't choose to become a full-time stripper. The luster of it is starting to dull, and I've been considering quitting. I believe my efforts could be used to do something more meaningful than increasing my family's wealth."

I nodded.

"I'm glad you recognize that you can do so much more, be so much more. Maybe one day you'll decide to become what you want and not what your family has decided for you. Often, it's those who have the least that do the most. With your family and status, you can create a movement, inspire a generation, build a better world."

Silence filled the cab of the car, and I didn't know if he'd taken offense to my comments or not, but I wasn't the type to care about someone's feelings, especially when they had enough power to do so much more than chase money.

"You're right. I can do better, could have been doing better, but I've allowed my parents to dictate a large chunk of my life. However, in the last few years, I think I have been slowly transitioning into who I believe I need to become."

"That's great."

I stared around, bending forward in the seat to get a good look at our surroundings.

"Where the heck are we?"

"You said you wanted to be surprised, so you'll have to wait and see," he said, his tone playful.

I didn't reply but stared at the big warehouse without a name or any identifying sign.

Night hadn't fully swallowed up the day, and the skyline, although painted with beautiful shrieks of red and orange, didn't make the building look any less haunted.

The size of this place alone was enough to make me question what the owner could possibly be keeping in there that required that much space. The place had to have been about a mile wide.

I glanced at Atlas, my pinched brows, setting up the question I wanted to ask.

"You're not taking me to some crazy ass white people shit, where I'll end up having to run and fight for my life while they hunt me down like big-game?" I asked.

His outburst of laughter stopped me from continuing what I considered legitimate questions.

"No, I'm not taking you to some white people shit. I'm taking you to a place I have a feeling you'll enjoy and appreciate."

"Um. Hum," I muttered, doubting I'd appreciate a warehouse the size of a small planet sitting out in the middle of nowhere. I couldn't even see the city lights in the distance from this location, indicating that we were way outside of anything that resembled civilization.

Atlas parked but didn't hop out of the car right away.

"Give me your wrist, please," he said while reaching into the center console and taking out two purple wristbands.

Reluctantly, and after a side eye and a few more expressive eyes for extra emphasis, I handed him my wrist.

He took it, his warm fingers sliding around it with a delicate caress. He lifted my wrist to his lips, kissing the inside with a smooth press that sent a tingle dancing up my arm before it raced down my spine.

My initial intention was to pull away, but I didn't. I didn't want to address how much I enjoyed his lips on my skin. He placed the purple band against the inside and turned my wrist to snap it into place. I took my arm back, glancing at my wrist that still held some of the warmth from his kiss.

When I glanced up, he was watching me with quiet amusement flashing in his gaze. The reaction disappeared when our eyes locked in a collision of curiosity. Neither of us moved. Something strong and imposing had us transfixed in this moment.

We continued to search each other's gazes. For purpose? For understanding? I wasn't sure.

A smile tugged at the corners of his lips, shone through his entrancing eyes, and enticed my lips to follow suit.

What the hell were we doing? Why were we sitting here acting crazy with these stupid smiles on our faces? I hadn't been high since high school, so why was I doing high people shit all of a sudden?

"Are we getting out?" I finally asked, pushing through the weird sensations that were riding me hard.

He nodded before hopping out and walking around the car. I sat there, still looking around with a scrunched-up nose, before he opened my door and reached his hand inside to help me out. I surprised myself by offering my hand, allowing his smooth vibe to ease the tension clinging to me for no reason.

We walked through the parking lot that was relatively empty, with no more than twenty cars in a lot that could hold hundreds.

"Is this place open?" I asked, knowing the answer but needing something to say.

"Of course, it's open. It's couples only tonight, so there won't be any waiting or large crowds."

"Perfect Energy," I read on the small engraved sign secured at the top of the door frame. The large white brick building was a few stories high in the front, but I had

noticed from the car that the back of the building rose to at least six or seven stories high.

Before I could ask what was inside again, the front door cracked open, and a couple walked out laughing. Their voices were laced with the excitement of whatever they had experienced inside this place.

"Hello," the couple greeted in unison. "You guys are going to have a great time," the guy said, giving us the thumbs up as they continued to walk past us.

A glance back showed the guy placing his hand around his woman's waist before he pulled her into his side and kissed the top of her head. Her girlish giggle and the squeeze she gave his ass when she placed her arm around him said that they were about to go and get busy, maybe even in their car.

More so than ever, I wanted to know what was inside this place. Atlas pulled open the oversized front door that resembled something from a Disney show. He swept his hand inside for me to enter first. I stepped through the door and was immediately stopped in my tracks.

Bells. Whistles. Flashing lights. Wind-tossed flags. Dancing lights. Cheering couples celebrating a victory they had won at a basketball shooting booth.

A rock-climbing wall off in the distance promised more entertainment. This place housed an impressive variety of different types of adult fun. There was paintball shooting, a war games chamber, and an arcade with a large see-through window that enticed you to come inside and play. A haunted house passed across my view, as well as several virtual reality rooms that promised things like gravity-free and other real-time experiences.

The open area we stood in had various equipment, like a boxing ring, an octagon for kickboxing, and a spring jump contraption. Everything in this place was meant to elicit fun and make you forget about whatever reality stressed you the hell out.

An exhilarating rush washed over me, enticing a wide smile. I had never been to anything like this, not even as a kid.

My childhood was all about trying to keep up with my brothers and hiding most of the trouble I'd gotten into at school from them and my father. No one had time to take me to parks and playgrounds, not even a measly visit to the state fair when it rolled into town.

My father was too busy working to feed and keep a roof over our heads after our mother was killed, and my brothers were too busy chasing girls to have time to do anything with their pesky little sister.

A tingly spike of energy kicked up my pulse. This place was breathing some type of new energy into me that I didn't know existed.

"You're smiling," Atlas noted.

"I was the kid growing up who never got to do anything fun like this," I replied. My leg jumped from how anxious I was to climb or kick something, and my fingers were tingling to shoot, slap, or tug on something.

"What are we doing first?" I questioned, my eyes dancing over the spectacular scenes laid out in front of me.

"Whatever you want," Atlas replied.

A bungee jump arena was off to the right, allowing you to be lifted into a tiny booth at least five stories high. You were then strapped into a rope where you decided to jump forward or backward or as a couple.

My eyes zeroed in on a couple making their way up the enormous rock-climbing wall in the distance. This place was vast enough for the wall to be at least a football field away.

I lifted and stuck my arm out, aiming my finger at the wall that rose at least five stories high.

"That. I want to see how far I make it. Believe it or not, I don't even know if I'm afraid of heights."

His brow lifted high on his forehead.

"You don't?"

I shook my head. "I've never done anything that would allow me to test myself."

"You really didn't get to play a lot when you were a kid, did you?" Atlas asked.

"No, and I think that's why I already like this place. I don't care if I can successfully do anything here, but the idea that I get to try excites me most."

"With that attitude, you are about to have a blast," he stated. His smile was laced with the same exhilaration I was experiencing.

He took my hand, and I didn't pull it away when he led us toward the back of the vast indoor adult theme park. There was no other way to describe this place.

The name on the outside, Perfect Energy, made sense now. The purple bracelets we were wearing were what people were passing in front of scanners to unlock some of the rides, rooms, and activities.

My head lifted higher on our approach to the wall, where an attendant waited with an inviting smile. Ropes and hooks dangled from various parts of his body.

"Welcome. Are you guys interested in climbing the wall tonight?"

"Yes," Atlas and I answered.

"What are your names?" he asked, his gaze moving from me to Atlas.

"I'm Atlas, and this is my lovely wife, Dayton."

My head whipped around so fast that my neck popped. Atlas was fighting to keep from laughing at my reaction. The attendant, Mike, according to his nametag, had such a sincere smile on his face at Atlas's lie that I didn't want to mess it up, so I kept my smart comment to myself.

"You two are a gorgeous couple, but how competitive are you with each other?"

"Very," I answered for the both of us. "I usually beat him at everything, so sometimes, I let him win so his ego can survive the dragging I'll usually put it through."

"Ouch," Atlas replied to my insult.

"Those are fighting words," Mike said. "It looks like we might have some true competition here tonight."

It took us a good ten to twelve minutes to go through the safety rules and get strapped into the ropes and protective gear. We looked to be truly ready to go mountain climbing.

Mike pointed out several cameras that filmed and snapped pictures at varying angles during our experience, leaving us unbothered about documenting our experience. The convenience of having them take photos and film certain portions of the activities allowed you to enjoy yourself to the fullest.

Mike took his time, showing each of us a path we could take to reach whatever goal we wanted to set for ourselves. My aim was to reach the top. However, not knowing if I was afraid of heights or not left me curious about how far I would actually go.

"Are you ready?" Atlas asked, his keen eyes amplifying the sincerity of his smile. I got the feeling that he didn't get a lot of play time when he was younger, either.

"Yes. Straight to the top!" I shouted enthusiastically.

"To the top," he repeated, reaching out his closed hand until I bumped my fist against his.

Mike's smile widened at our show of sportsmanship. I glanced up at two more attendants, one at the top of the wall and one more about halfway up in case we needed a lifeline, up or down.

"Go!" Mike exclaimed excitedly while cheering us on.

The one word had my heart beating faster, and my adrenaline spiked the moment my hand gripped the first notch.

Five minutes in and about two stories up, I hit an area where it was a long stretch, plus I had to bend back to reach the next notch. There wasn't anywhere to place my damn feet. I bit into my lips, contemplating my next move.

Atlas was a few pegs higher than me, but I knew, without a doubt, he was waiting for me. The gesture made me glance over and smile my appreciation in his direction when I wasn't straining, gasping, stretching, and climbing.

I wasn't going to let this inanimate structure beat me. I dropped back down a few pegs and took a different route that led me to the third level before my muscles began to burn. Glancing down at the floor and seeing the view at this higher angle didn't bother me. It answered my question of whether or not I was afraid of heights.

Atlas had taken a route that drew him close enough to me for us to talk back and forth.

"You're almost there, Dayton. Don't think about anything but that big yellow flag you will be pulling when you defeat this wall," he encouraged.

I nodded.

"Defeat the wall," I chanted before reaching up and gripping the next notch.

I didn't notice I was at the top until a step up showed me that the wall was no longer in my face. A dash of cool air hit my face first before it swooshed against my body. A smile baring all my teeth formed as my shaky legs and jelly arms got me over the top of the wall that was a few feet wide.

"You're a badass, you know that?" Atlas yelled. Pride rang as heavy in his tone as it did in his expression. He pointed down at the floor where Mike was waving up at us.

"Look at what you did?" he said excitedly, lifting his hands and pumping into the air. I mimicked his actions, celebrating our victory—one I never saw coming, never even knew I needed to accomplish. The stress of my everyday life was covered, buried under this big fluffy cloud of joy coursing through me.

***

Atlas

The smile on Dayton's face was worth more money than I could ever make. It was something to be cherished and memorized. I reveled in the way she threw her head back and allowed her laughter to pour out freely. There was a girlish charm attached to the sound.

It had been a long time since I'd been the reason someone smiled a genuine smile. It was addicting, and I was willing to do just about anything to keep her laughing just like that.

Once we were safely off the wall and untangled from the ropes, we thanked Mike and waved at the rest of the wall people before stepping off in no general direction, still giggling from our adventure.

"So, what do you want to do next? Are you hungry? We can get snacks here, but if you want to get something later, we can," I said, willing to do and go wherever she wanted.

"I'm not hungry. There's too much to do," she replied, glancing around with a buzz of excitement spilling from her, warm and intoxicating.

We walked and took in all the places and activities offered, stopping twice to contemplate our next adventure. She considered the maze, with a starting point inside and extending outside the building. According to the legend, there was even a small body of water that ran through a portion of the maze that you had to memorize before entering it.

She lost interest in the maze, allowing something else to call her attention. Her eyes zeroed in on a set of cars on a life-sized poster.

"Can we race next?"

"Of course we can," I replied, lifting my armband to her eye level. "We can do anything in this building, including hopping on a plane to do the real-life skydive adventure they offer."

"You're kidding," she said, lips parted and eyes wide. She paused to contemplate the news.

"I don't think I'm ready to sling myself from a perfectly good plane. For now, I do like the way these life-size cars look on this display."

I took her hand and led her toward the area she had pointed out at the left back of the building.

"I can't wait until we experience this one," I told her, kissing the back of her hand. This feeling she helped to create within me, this warm, buzzing rush, was one I never wanted to go away.

We raced on the outdoor track that passed several miles through a patch of woods in the back of the complex. This time wasn't like on the wall. I didn't have to wait for Dayton because she drove like a bat out of hell, forcing me to keep up with her.

She dashed around dangerous curves and took hills, dips, and tight corners like she'd been trained by Mario Andretti himself. Exhilaration flowed like liquid fire charging through my veins.

Fifteen minutes later.

"You think you have room for one more activity?" I asked after she'd won the race and was carrying her trophy.

She paused, the smile in her gaze meeting mine. "I think I can do more than one more. This is the kind of let-my-hair-down moment I've been needing."

"Good," I told her, feeding off her enthusiasm and enjoying the adult fun that made this one of the best nights I had enjoyed in a long time.

I didn't get to take Dayton home with me, but I didn't need to. This date marked a turning point in our lives and allowed us to create a foundation of something special that we could continue to build on. This night was our beginning.

Chapter Eleven

Dayton

Charlene cracked the door open, her smile as warm a greeting as the hug she pulled me into. "This kind of feels like you miss me," I said, returning her hug before easing back and looking into her face. "What's that young man been doing to you up in this spot?" I questioned her playfully.

When she discovered that Ransome was younger than she assumed, she was stressed at first, until he made her see that it didn't matter.

The big smile on her face right now said it all. She had recently moved into her new place, and this was her housewarming dinner. Callie and I were the only guests at this party. Occasionally, we hung out with other women, but for the most part, we kept our circle tight.

"This is nice," I said, mimicking Tiffany Haddish's character while referring to her new place. The doorbell rang and Charlene welcomed Callie.

Callie walked up to me and placed a caring arm around my waist, an action I returned with a tight squeeze. I released Callie and continued my quest, showing myself around Charlene's new three-bedroom condo.

"I'll fix us some drinks," Charlene stated, walking toward the bar area near her dining room.

After I checked out the downstairs area and picked up my drink, I took the stairs up to explore the second level. The place highlighted Charlene's impressive decorating skills. She and Callie had taken pity on me and got together to decorate my condo a few years ago. My skills in that area were lacking, and I had no desire to improve them.

"It looks like I'm going to have a beautiful place to crash if I get too drunk," I called to Charlene.

"You sure will," she returned, chuckling.

When she was with her ex, she would spend nights with Callie and me, but we couldn't stand Charlene's ex, Carter, so staying at her old place was out of the question. Despite my teasing him about being a stripper and younger than Charlene, Ransome treated her like she was his whole world and kept her smiling.

I strolled back into the living room and fell onto the large, comfy leather couch next to Callie. The spread of cheeses, chocolates, and enough finger foods to put me into a temporary coma sat atop the coffee table.

I sipped from my second drink that Charlene had conveniently set in place. My brain was keyed up and ready to receive the latest and greatest gossip. With both my friends dating strippers now, I expected a lot of it to be spewing from them.

Lifting my arm, I glanced down at my watch. Ten whole minutes and cricket sounds chirped in my head versus the melodramatic reports about relationship dramas. I would venture to say that strippers weren't like they used to be. All I was getting was idle chitchat that may as well have been white noise.

The silence. *Why was it so quiet?* My eyes darted back and forth between Charlene, sitting on the loveseat adjacent to us, and Callie, sitting next to me.

"Why the hell are you two looking at me like you found a crack pipe in my pocket, and you're about to start my intervention?"

"We know what you've been up to," Callie stated, her tone accusatory.

How the hell did they know about Atlas?

I squinted. I'm sure, confusion rested in the creases of my face. Me and Atlas hadn't even slept with each other yet, and I damn sure wasn't looking to make him my man.

"You've been putting yourself in danger again," Charlene stated, eyeballing me like the mother hen she was. "I admire the way you fight for women, our rights, and especially abused women, but you can't save everyone, and you can't keep putting yourself between an angry man and the woman they intend to take that anger out on."

Crisis avoided. Tension relieved. They weren't talking about Atlas.

"How do you know what I've been up to? Did you inherit a couple of Carter's security guards when he went to jail and have them follow me or something?" I asked, flashing her a wicked side-eye.

"I don't need security to know what you're up to," Charlene countered. "When it's hard for either of us to get you on the phone or when you rush us off the phone. When you don't have any snappy comebacks or teasing remarks, it all says you're working on something that could get you hurt or in trouble. If you have to take action, you need to get us to help you."

Although I knew the offer was genuine, the discipline in Charlene's tone made me feel like a kid getting fussed at by her mother.

"I understand what you're saying, and I know without a doubt that you two will be the first in line to help me. However, I can't consciously put you in danger. The same way you didn't tell us about Carter's trifling ass right away to protect us is why I don't want you involved. If something happened to one of you, I won't be okay. Trouble will be an understatement for what the city would see."

We were at a crossroads. They wanted to help me in my fight to help women who came to me when they had no one else, but it was bad enough that I was risking myself. I didn't want to place them in danger if things went bad. We sat in silence, each second crawling by like a minute while we sipped our drinks.

"When was the last time you went to Quiet Chaos?" Charlene finally questioned, providing us the subject change we needed.

Although I wasn't looking in her direction, I could sense Callie's eyes on me. I rolled my eyes at Charlene's ass and sent a wicked side-eye in Callie's direction.

"You mean the club where both your men work? Do you think I want to go there and watch *your* men take off their clothes? You two know better than anyone, once I get a little liquor in me, I don't give a damn who they belong to. If they are on that stage, shaking their shit for the public, all bets are off. My money is going into a G-string, and a dick will get stroked."

Their faces squeezed into disgusted knots.

"You are ruthless. And gutter," Charlene stated teasingly. She knew damn well Ransome and Trent were frogs to me the moment I found out they were dating my friends. They weren't just any frogs either—they were those ugly-ass spotted ones that were covered in warts. Even if shit didn't work out for them, Ransome and Trent were as good as eunuchs to me.

"Can we change the subject?" Callie stated.

My head shook. "No, let's not change the subject. This is something that should be discussed. Dating a man who gets naked for random women is not easy, and your thoughts on the matter should not be silenced. Let that shit out. This is a safe space. Say whatever's on your mind," I advised her.

She swallowed hard, the stress lines between her eyes visible. Dating Trent wasn't easy for her, but she and he had somehow found a way back to each other after a brief fling over a year ago, so something was going right.

"Now, go on and tell Dr. Dayton how you feel," I urged, glancing at them both when silence invaded our space. "Charlene, you first since you put us on this path when you decided to date Ransome. How's he been treating you? Are you having any second thoughts about dating a man of the stage?"

Callie's laugh sounded at my comment, and Charlene lifted a finger while fighting not to laugh.

"Technically, Callie started this journey we're on when she was sneaking around in New York with Trent a year ago," she said.

Charlene thought she was slick. All she was doing was attempting to remove the spotlight from her. Nevertheless, our eyes landed on Callie, who closed her eyes and let her chin drop to her chest. After a few moments, she lifted her head with renewed strength in her gaze.

"Trent is like two different people. He's caring, attentive, and thoughtful in a way that makes me want to glue myself to him. Then there's the version of him who dances. He pours his heart and soul into his performances, and although he would probably never admit it, I think he enjoys it. It's hard to think about that side of him without my mind going down avenues I don't want it going in," Callie said.

Her mind was going down some of those avenues now, based on how she stared straight ahead.

"Do I like what Trent does for a living? Heck no, I don't like it at all. I hate thinking about those women with their hands all over him, some angling to take him home, some throwing themselves at him." She aimed a finger at her chest. "We were those women not too long ago, so I know what they see and, in most cases, what they're thinking. I trust him because he hasn't given me a reason not to, but on the nights that he has to dance, all types of shit goes through my head."

I rubbed a caring hand up and down her forearm.

"I can only imagine the stress you feel. But he's not going to be in it much longer, right?" I questioned, remembering her saying something about him preparing to put his education to work and quit dancing.

She nodded absently.

"Yes. He said one more year to pay off his house and pad his savings, and then he'll be free to pursue his dream of being his own boss."

"I'm not trying to question your man's integrity, but do you believe him when he says he's going to quit in a year?" I asked, voicing a question I'd want an answer to if I were in the same situation.

"Yes, I do. He's been working hard over the years to finally kickstart the career he's enthusiastic about beginning. You don't invest that kind of time and money into something you only have a fleeting interest in. And he is much smarter than some women, me included, gave him credit for. Sometimes I believe it messes with his head when he knows he's not being taken seriously because of how he looks," Callie stated.

"In that aspect, I can empathize with him. Women, especially black women, aren't taken seriously in some situations and environments. If I had a dollar for every time I'm mistaken for the administrative assistant or a personal assistant instead of one of the company's top accountants, I'd be rich," Charlene stated.

"Richer," I corrected her. She always downplayed her income, and I think it had a lot to do with her ex, Carter's, ego. I don't think he had a clue as to how much Charlene made a year. She brought home more than him, "sitting behind a desk," as he called it, even though he was running his own successful security company with over sixty employees. She smiled at my comment.

"Be proud of what you've accomplished. You worked hard for your career. I know your ass is clocking over a quarter million a year plus bonuses. Why do you think I'm friends with you," I said teasingly.

I deserved the hard slap she delivered to my forearm for that one. I glanced at Callie, casting the spotlight back in her direction.

"I don't think you have anything to worry about. Trent looks at you the same way Ransome looks at Charlene, all starry-eyed like he's been hypnotized or something. Nose wide open."

We chuckled at that one.

"Charlene, how are you feeling about your little young tender?" I asked her, a teasing smirk resting on my lips.

"He may be young, but that man was ready," she said, shaking her head at a memory I did not want the details about.

"He isn't intimidated about how much I make. I can talk about work with him, and he actually listens, although he has no idea what I'm talking about most of the time. But what matters is that he gets that it matters to me. It bothers me that he dances, but I reason with myself that he's working. It's his job, not his life. As Callie mentioned about her with Trent, I misjudged Ransome when we first met. I honestly didn't see him as anything but a temporary fix to my problem. He showed me better than I allowed myself to conclude that he was smart, that he had goals and dreams outside the club, and was working hard to achieve them. I'm proud of him, and I let him know it. As black women, we know how it feels not to be appreciated, so I let him know as often as I can that I see his efforts and that I'm proud of him. And if I'm being honest, he was the one who taught me to appreciate myself more. He's young, but he's one of the best things to ever happen to me as far as understanding, affection, and communication goes. I don't like that he dances, but I will let him decide when he's ready to stop."

I stared at her, seeing something new within her that I hadn't seen before. Since Ransome came into her life, she'd been more outspoken and happy, like he injected a big dose of life into her veins.

"You love him, don't you?" I asked, half joking and half serious although I already knew the answer.

I was a little bit jealous, but there was no way I couldn't be happy for Charlene. She deserved a good man, especially after that ancient alien she'd been with for a decade who cheated and treated her like she was a pet he wanted to keep in the house and let out and walk whenever he had time.

"Yes. I love him," she said, her face lighting up.

"I'm happy for you. You know that. Genuinely happy for the both of you," I said, reaching out and taking their hands."

I was never the one to get emotional, but for reasons I hadn't picked through yet, my friend's news pulled harder at my heartstrings than usual.

"Atlas," the sneaky ass little voice in my head had the nerve to point out.

Chapter Twelve

Dayton

I had serious doubts about seeing Atlas again, but here I was, sharing a space with him once more. At his penthouse, no less. The apartment was located in the building he worked out of. Therefore, it was like we were at a hotel rather than his place of residence.

How did this happen?

I believed the talk I had with Charlene and Callie a few days ago had inspired me to be a little more receptive to Atlas's advances.

"Dance?" I questioned after he'd made the out-of-the-blue suggestion. We were supposed to be having dinner, but I knew damn well that food wasn't the only thing that would be offered up between us.

"You want to dance with me? Right now?"

I glanced at my half empty plate of food and the beautiful sight of the second glass of wine he'd poured us. Besides, the man could actually cook real food, from scratch that tasted good.

He nodded while walking around his table toward me. He reached out, and I took his hand, standing and allowing him to lead me into the living room. He picked up a remote and turned the music up. My smile widened at the sound of *Lollipop*, the instrumental version.

His hand slid, warm and gentle, around my waist before he pulled me in close. There was no use in me pretending I didn't like it, but I was too damn stubborn to admit to him and myself that I enjoyed his company.

We vibed, swaying to the beat and allowing the rhythm to flow through us along with the indelible connection I'd been trying hard to deny. The warm flow of the dance surrounded me as much as Atlas's strong arms and body.

I leaned in, allowing my head to rest against his strong shoulder when a slow jam came on. The position made him tighten his hold and embrace me with the type of caress that offered support, security, and care. All the things I desired but could never get a man to give me freely, yet Atlas was covering all the bases in an impromptu dance. This was too good to be true and, therefore, left me reluctant and guarding my feelings.

He pulled me in tighter, pushing away my doubt and forcing me to let our chemistry flow.

"Thank you for agreeing to see me again," he whispered into my hair.

"You can be a very convincing man, but you have to be in order to contend with my strong personality," I replied truthfully, glancing up at him.

"You are a beautiful woman, and although that is what initially got my attention, it was the close-up views of you that drove my desire to know more about you. Your drive to fight for what's right. The way you care about your friends and other women. The way you allow yourself to have fun without restraint. You're witty. You're smart. I enjoy every aspect of you, Dayton."

He was making me blush, and though I tried, I failed to keep a grin from bursting free.

"Thank you," I told him before placing a light kiss, barely a brush of my lips, over his clean-shaven cheek. His eyes caught mine before I resumed my position. Like the few times before, we were caught in one of our chemistry-induced trances. This time, I didn't force myself out of it.

I stared into his eyes, deep enough to see that Atlas genuinely cared about me. There were no ulterior motives, no game-playing. He leaned in, close enough for us to share breathing space, our eyes still penetrating each other's, searching.

His hands were gliding along my back and side, not in a sexual way, but to caress me better. His hold on me helped me muddle through the swarm of emotions that were attacking me, the building intensity stealing away my breath.

We leaned into our kiss, meeting in a soft, inviting push before my tingling lips rolled over the wet warmth of his with a need for more. We pressed harder, our lips parting, our tongues sensually sliding over each other's before we slipped into a delicate dance.

This kiss lingered, lasted, and stirred emotions our bodies could no longer ignore, hide, or pretend weren't there. I moaned against his mouth, unable to keep the energizing radiance that the kiss had stirred from bursting free.

One of Atlas's hands cupped my cheek and squeezed, the other went around my back, pulling me into him. I slid my arms around his neck, pulling him closer to me.

I couldn't get him close enough, no matter how tightly I squeezed my arms around his neck or how firmly I pressed my lips into his. He broke the kiss, his breathing erratic, his heavy-lidded eyes pinned on mine and searching while I did the same.

My face tensed, but it wasn't because I was upset. Why had he pulled away? I wanted more. Needed it to help me cut through this thick, intoxicating tension.

"I think it goes without saying, but I'll say it anyway. We have…"

I couldn't think of the right word to describe it.

"Chemistry," he finished for me. It was the perfect word to describe what we were sharing, but he and I both knew that there was a bit more than chemistry going on between us. This was like nothing I'd ever experienced or ever knew existed.

I reached up and pulled his face back down to mine, recapturing the invigorating energy and buzz that awakened every cell and powered through my blood with a relentless force. This time, neither of us pulled away until we were gasping.

My chest heaved against his. His hands were filled with my ass as I was scratching at his side to pull his shirt out of his pants. My frantic movement spurred him to go for my shirt. Before I knew it, he'd found a way to work the top up my body while giving me hot kisses and using his tongue to paint pleasure along my neck and shoulders.

The way he gripped my ass and my tits, squeezing and manipulating my flesh through my clothes, had me hot and needy. Seeing that big bulge in his pants drew my attention, and when we went in for another kiss, I allowed my hands to feel, measure, and explore.

"Shit," he breathed against my lips before reaching down and squeezing my hand harder around his dick. I'd hoped he wasn't one of those stocking stuffers when I'd seen him dance at the club.

Atlas was packing enough in those pants that he would probably have my ass running from him. I smiled against his lips. I wanted to be chased, especially with the kind of equipment he would be threatening me with.

We inched back until my back was pushed up against the cold surface of the wall. He reached down and nudged my pants down. I helped, wiggling my way out of them while enjoying the smooth press of his lips to my legs all the way down until he stripped my pants and heels off my feet.

His hands glided back up and the glint in his eyes while trailing the movement was as palpable as his caress. His look, an edgy, I'm-about-to-fuck-you-to-sleep expression radiating from his eyes, had me leaking uncontrollably. He kissed right above my panty line, making me rub my knees together to control my eagerness.

He placed his hands together before bringing them forward until they were pushing between my thighs and getting me to spread my legs. Once my legs were spread to where he wanted them, he slid his hand over my inner thighs and turned them around.

"Aww!" I yelled when he deadlifted me, my back sliding up the wall and legs held in his tight grip. I wasn't a lightweight woman. I was five-six and one-seventy. Depending on who was doing the measuring, I was thick to some, medium to some, and large-framed to others.

Atlas lifted me up this wall like I was a snack versus a full meal. With my legs over his shoulders and his breath on my pussy, I had nowhere to go and no complaints to make. And that flaming gaze he shot up at me told me he knew it too.

He didn't ask permission or even hint at what he was about to do. He slipped my panties to the side and put his tongue to work.

"Oh, shit," slipped out on a quick shaky breath. Being eaten at this high elevation was a sexual fantasy I never knew I needed. I gripped Atlas's head for support, but it didn't stop him from controlling how wide he wanted my legs and how vigorously or expressively he used his tongue.

I didn't know how much time had passed, but I forgot about how high I was hiked up in the air. I was now thrusting and doing my best to ride the man's face. I should have been afraid of falling because my only safety net was his hands gripping my legs and the wall at my back.

However, the ravenous flow of my desire ate all my fears and concerns.

My moans were about as out of control as my erratic breaths and thrusting movements against that wall. When he eased his head back enough to glance up at me, I saw his tongue licking up and down my clit with slow wet swipes that made my damn left eye start twitching along with my inner thighs.

"Oh. Fuck. Atlas," I moaned low in my throat while tightening the grip I had on his hair and right shoulder, my nails digging in deep.

"I'm…"

It was all I managed before my head fell back against the wall, and I melted. I swore this man made my pussy dissolve on his tongue while wave after wave of pure pleasure exploded through me, possessed me, and owned me.

If there was a class to be given on how to give a woman a master orgasm, Atlas needed to be teaching it because…damn. We hadn't even had sex yet, and his oral was better than most of the sex I had experienced, and that was saying something.

He didn't ease me down right away either—he lowered me after the shaking stopped. I peeled my eyes open when my feet touched the floor. My knees were about as shaky as warm Jell-O, but my eyes were pinned on Atlas.

When I bent my shaky knees for a taste of him, he stopped me with a shake of his head.

"You can do that later. Right now, I have to fuck you, or I might explode in these pants."

"Oh," I said, grinning. He was ready to sample the goods he'd just devoured, and I didn't plan on stopping him.

"Let me help you out of this," I offered, undoing his belt before he could answer. He played a game of tug of war with my nipples after relieving me of my bra. I probably would have been moaning if I hadn't been so damn distracted by what was coming up out of those pants and briefs.

"Hello, Mr. Sir," I said, giving him a name right away. Mr. Sir was about as thick and long as my forearm, and I swore he was talking to me, whispering shit about how he would give my pussy a workout.

"Yes, you are," I replied to the dick, forgetting all about getting those pants the rest of the way down Atlas's toned legs. Admiring it, I ran my hands up and down the thick length. Damn, this man was blessed. I didn't even know if I could take Mr. Sir, but I believe my hungry ass cat was willing to give it a good try.

I bent, taking his pants down in a flash while eyeing his dick and licking my lips. I couldn't help myself. I leaned forward and kissed it. I even did the hand gesture, pointing my fingers at my eyes before aiming them back at him, letting him know that I saw him, and I respected what he was promising to do to me.

"Are you two finished talking? Can I get some attention, too?" Atlas asked, forcing me to smile while I ripped my eyes away from my new lover.

I gasped when I collided with Atlas's hard chest, and he put a kiss on me that brought my noodled knees right back.

"How do you want it?" he asked against my lips before he reached down and gripped my dripping pussy, moving his finger around my wet lips until he was able to slip two fingers inside me.

"Any way you want to deliver it," I replied while he was backing my ass up. To where, I didn't care. He had me in a way I had never been before, ready to jump his ass if we didn't start fucking soon.

While I was jumping out of my drenched panties, he reached down, scooped up his pants, and pulled his wallet from the back pocket before dropping them. He pulled a condom from his wallet, still walking to keep backing my ass up. A low, "Oh," flew out of my mouth when the backs of my legs struck something solid.

The chaise. *Good.* The solid piece of furniture was long and wide enough to accommodate both of us.

Atlas placed the condom between his lips and ripped open the wrapper while placing his free hand atop my shoulder and guiding me down. My eyes were trained on how expertly he was working that condom up his length with one hand while eye-fucking me.

I was so busy watching him I fell onto the side of the chaise, my eyes still on his hands working up and down his dick. I reached up and took over the job, believing that this man's dick had the power to possess.

He shoved me back, and I laid there, diagonal to the furniture, part of my left shoulder against the arm on the other side. The positioning left enough room for Atlas to climb between my legs on his knees. He pushed his left leg up under my right thigh, spreading my legs wider, while he controlled my left leg with a tight grip on my inner thigh.

He didn't lean over me, either. Atlas lifted my lower body enough to meet him halfway. My neck stretched hard to see. All I saw were love stars flaring off between my pussy and the big pink dick coming down to her.

The first hot lick kissed my clit and poked at my wet, throbbing hole. He pushed teasingly, inching into me with a slow firmness that had my leg jumping in his hand. My heart pumped fast, and my breaths grew ragged, attempting to keep up with the pace.

I hummed the moan, transfixed on where he was sliding between my brown lips and stretching me open to accommodate him.

"At last," I gasped when he sank himself all the way in, allowing me to see the whole sexy ass process. He backed halfway out and pushed back inside. He repeated the delicious stroking until I fully accepted him with a slick wetness I had never achieved. My mouth dropped open, and my moans turned into a song.

"Your pussy is magic," he spat out while watching how he was burying himself inside me.

"Tell me I can have more before the sun rises," he said.

My belly quivered, my thighs shook, my legs were spread wider, and I took every deep grinding thrust until the tension left my body, and Atlas was fucking me without any resistance. I didn't even notice when I'd taken a grip of the velvety upholstery covering the chaise until it snapped out of my tight grip. My other hand was digging into the tight flexing of abdominal muscles.

"Oh fuck, right there," I muttered, not sure if my moaning was the understandable words of encouragement I intended.

"More before the sun rises," Atlas repeated his demand, peppering each hard thrust with a word.

"Yes. Fuck, yes!" I yelled. "You can have as much as you want."

What the hell was I saying? This was supposed to be a one-and-done type of situation. Wasn't it? But, he was fucking me so good it was hard to say no to him already securing our second round.

The way I was breathing, I needed a paper bag to blow into. The foot of the leg he had his muscular thigh tucked under was flapping around in the air. He had pinned the other leg back so high, it allowed him to go deep enough for his dick to blow oxygen into my lungs.

"Atlas. Oh. Atlas," I exclaimed, observing him through one eye because the other was twitching so badly. This man was road-mapping my pussy with directions on how to find his dick anywhere in the continental United States.

"You. You…" was all I could manage.

"Yes, baby. What?" he questioned.

"I'm. You."

He must have noticed that I was too overwhelmed for proper speech.

"This can be yours whenever and however you want it. Now, I need you to come on my dick, hard. I want to feel every last juicy drop."

With that, I went berserk, coming apart while my mind reached out to the stars for guidance. The pounding thrust was so fucking delicious that my mouth dropped open, and a little drool actually slipped out of the corner.

This was a new experience for me. An orgasm that took me on a journey where my body and mind were both blown and filled with a bliss-kissed adventure I had never experienced. I couldn't tell you if I was breathing right then or holding my breath. I didn't care. I was free, perfect, at peace, and safe.

"Dayton. Baby. Fuck," Atlas yelled, meeting his own orgasmic maker.

At thirty years old, I had finally experienced *The Orgasm*. The best of my life. Atlas Belair had given me the gift without any freak show tricks or sideshow theatrics but with good old-fashioned fucking.

Coming out of the best high of my life didn't feel odd. It was freeing, like something I'd been waiting to have unlocked had finally been released.

Atlas eased out of me slowly, our eyes remaining on each other. He and I both knew that this was only the beginning. Our sex was explosive and something that you didn't do once.

I could already picture us fucking every chance we got until we grew tired of each other. It was hard to picture getting bored of sex that damn good, but it was the only outcome for us.

A smile teased my lips while I stared at him with all these ideas rolling through my head. He had opened Pandora's box, and I wanted to keep playing.

Chapter Thirteen

Atlas

Dayton had me in the kitchen at seven-thirty in the morning, cooking her breakfast. Although I knew how to cook a large variety of dishes, this was a task I had never even done for my ex-wife.

We'd had sex in every way imaginable. Still, when Dayton climbed on top of me and rode me into the afterlife, I swore I'd been sexually reborn.

"Umm," I groaned. My dick stirred from the afterthoughts. Considering that we had fucked five times in seven hours before we finally passed out, my dick was as exhausted as me, and we needed to replenish some of the energy we'd lost last night.

I wasn't even sure if there were enough eggs, toast, breakfast sausages, and coffee in this house right now that could restore us. The pitter-patter of size seven and a half feet called my attention away from turning the sausages before sexy light brown legs dragged me further away from my task.

"Smells good," she said, walking up next to me and glancing at our plates and the pot of freshly brewed coffee.

I scooped out a couple of sausages and dropped them onto her plate and a few onto mine before I cut the stove off and turned to face her. I didn't even have to ask. I bent, and our lips met in a lingering kiss that heated my blood.

Dayton was the most addictive woman I'd ever met. I knew it from the moment I spotted her, but being with her confirmed it for me. She was one of those women who made you not care if you got hurt in the relationship because she was worth it.

Once we broke the kiss, I sent a light slap across her ass before picking up one of the plates and a cup of coffee and handing it to her.

There's cream and sugar on the table if you want it," I told her before picking up my plate and coffee and joining her.

Small talk and roaming eyes traveled across the table. Things were going well until she licked that damn sausage.

"Why did you have to go and do that, Dayton?"

I swallowed hard and watched her devious smile widen. Seeing her tongue slide up the side of that piece of sausage set something off within me, and all I pictured was me fucking her.

Since the food was nearly done, I saw no reason we needed the dishes anymore. I swept my hand over the table, slowly and deliberately, so when the dishes fell to the floor, they didn't all crash and bang and spill the food and liquid at the same time and in the same place.

The sound of the mess I was making was music to my ears while my eyes feasted on Dayton. Her body was something from one of my dreams, lush, curvy, with a small waist and a round ass with the power to hypnotize.

Her skin was much lighter than I'd initially seen. Seeing her without her shirt and bra that first time had me doing a double-take at her tan lines. I was probably an idiot for thinking it, but I didn't know people of color tanned on purpose.

I wiggled my finger, calling Dayton closer. She took things up a notch, crawling atop the table and sliding over to me, clearing the last of the dishes and utensils out of our way.

"You called," she said, dropping her legs over the side of the table and sitting them in front of me. I eased between her legs, spreading them.

I loved seeing her in nothing but one of my button-ups that she pulled from the closet. We'd had a fuck session inside my walk-in last night when she had gone in there to find something to sleep in.

Her warm fingertips slid up my chest until she was able to sling her arms around my neck and pulled me closer.

"Spend the rest of the weekend with me," I suggested and begged at the same time.

Instead of answering, she tugged on my neck, closing the last few inches of space until our lips met.

The kiss dragged on slowly, but like I had learned last night, our chemistry heated fast and burned with a possessive passion that neither of us could control. My eager fingers climbed up her bare legs until I was able to cup her supple cheeks. I used one hand to shove my shorts down, freeing myself.

"Damn. Condom," I said.

"Don't worry," she told me, reaching into the pocket of my shirt that she wore and taking one out. "I came to this table to eat, to be eaten, and to get stuffed."

"My kind of woman," I whispered against her lips while she worked on rolling that condom over my achingly hard dick.

No sooner than she slid it on did I pull her to the edge of the table and push into her.

"Aww," we both exhaled loudly on the first spine-tingling thrust. She was already slick enough to take me most of the way in. I eased back and pushed forward until I was buried deep enough to make her legs shake.

She laid back on the table while I held her legs up and open. Seeing me sliding in and out of her slick pussy, and the way her sexy lower lips and silky pink center swallowed me was too much. I wasn't going to last, and based on the way she was thrusting against me and shouting my name, neither was she.

"Atlas. Don't stop. Deeper, baby," Dayton yelled.

A foreign noise invaded our session, throwing off my stroke, but I didn't dare stop. Again, the sound of a throat clearing invaded my consciousness.

I glanced up... "Oh, shit!" I yelled and stopped mid-stroke.

"Trent, I'm almost there. I told you not to stop!" Dayton yelled, thrusting her pussy against my still-hard dick.

"Holly, what the fuck are you doing in my house?" I yelled at the intruder.

My face was pulled into a tight knot of anger at my ex-wife standing about ten feet away from the table in the doorway that led into my kitchen.

Dayton glanced up and over her shoulder, but she kept her legs wrapped around my ass and back.

"This is a serious invasion of my privacy. I changed the locks. How did you get into my house?" I questioned, my face pinched in a mix of irritation and anger.

Dayton put her gaze on me. "This is your ex-wife?"

I nodded.

"And she's not supposed to be in your house?" she asked.

I nodded again, anger flaring my nostrils.

"In that case. Can we finish? That bitch can wait until the police arrive to take her out of here for breaking and entering."

I glanced down at Dayton, wide-eyed.

The seriousness etched in her gaze told me she wasn't joking. The fact that my dick was still inside her and hadn't gone down was a testament to how sexy she was. Not even my ex breaking into my house and watching us had tamped down the heat we created together.

Dayton nudged my ass with the heel of her foot, which caused me to shift against her. The slight movement made my dick move inside her and hyped up my fiery desire. Were we really about to keep fucking while my ex-wife stood and watched?

My body moved, and my mind followed. With my eyes on the beautiful, sexy woman displayed before me, I was able to tune my ex out while Dayton reached up and grabbed my ass, taking me in deeper. There was no way to stop now that I was balls deep inside her while her walls spread warm, wet magic around my shaft.

"Dayton. Fuck," I muttered while pumping in and out of her fast and hard. Our moans and grunts were in full effect. A quick glance up showed the ex-wife still standing there, fuming, with her arms crossed and mouth open as wide as her eyes.

"Oh! Atlas. You're the only one who can make me come this hard," Dayton said. "I'm glad this is my dick now, and this pussy is all for you."

"You are the best I ever had," I shouted, and it wasn't a lie. Dayton had the kind of sex that could drive a sane man like me mad and just crazy enough to keep fucking her while my ex stood there and watched.

"I'm coming. Oh, God. Atlas!" she yelled before she exploded into a pulsing inferno of moans and gasps. Her constricting walls squeezed my dick into submission, and I followed suit, shouting her name, shaking and shivering until I was lost in pleasure.

We came out of the haze of our lust together.

"I can't believe you two disrespectful ass people did that in front of me," Holly had the nerve to grit out. "I just wanted to talk to you."

I eased out of Dayton and reached to help her up before finding and jumping back into my shorts.

"If you need to talk to me for any reason, you pick up the phone and call. You don't come and break into my house."

"I didn't break in. The front door was open, so I walked in when I heard voices inside."

Holly was a good liar. I didn't believe I'd been careless enough to leave the front door open, but I would give her the benefit of the doubt.

"I called you three times this week. You never called me back. I decided to stop by," she said, checking out Dayton's naked body when I helped her off the table. She let her eyes linger and didn't put them back on me until Dayton gave her a wicked side-eye for staring.

"You like what you see, ex-wife? Is this why you two divorced—you prefer cats?" Dayton taunted.

"You have disrespected me enough. You will not talk to me that way. He will be done with the likes of you soon enough, and I'll never have to worry about seeing you again," Holly barked.

"What do you want, Holly? We have nothing to discuss. You got your settlement and a house out of me despite the prenup you broke by cheating, so what could we possibly need to discuss?"

"Can I talk to you in private, please?" she insisted, cutting her eyes at Dayton.

"Whatever you came here to say, you can say it in front of Dayton."

"We're pregnant," she blurted out.

I pursed my lips before releasing a peel of laughter.

"I haven't touched you in over three years, and our divorce was finalized for two and a half of those years. Unless you've figured out how to carry a baby for over three years, you, being pregnant by me, is not possible. And don't even think about trying to pin someone else's baby on me."

She glanced at Dayton before putting her eyes back on me. There was a satisfied smirk in her gaze.

"We were planning to do invitro fertilization since I had trouble conceiving, remember? We began the process, so the doctors had everything they needed from both of us. Instead of canning the project, I found a surrogate and finished the process," she announced with a wicked smirk on her face.

I took a few steps closer, fury flaring inside me. "You can't do that without my consent."

I shook my head, my eyes burning with a fury I'd never experienced before. Holly was the type to do some vile shit like this right when I was making an attempt to establish a relationship with Dayton.

"See, that's the thing, Atlas. I did have your consent. All of the paperwork you signed at the time was legal and binding, and since we never included any of it in our divorce proceedings, my lawyer informed me that I still had a right to have our baby.

Dayton stood by, watching this shit show while buttoning herself back into my shirt. I took another step closer to Holly, shaking my head and needing to get a good look into her eyes to see if she was using drugs. It was the one thing that could explain her being in my place uninvited and her spewing this craziness about having my baby years after our divorce had been finalized.

"Tell me you didn't do this. Tell me you wouldn't stoop so low to get back at me for divorcing you?"

She smiled, her expression laced with vicious intentions. I aimed a stiff finger at her.

"You were the one who fucked up our marriage, and you go and do this on top of it," I barked.

Her smile widened, increasing my anger to a level beyond my comprehension.

"You wanted our baby, too, despite what happened to us. And now, it's on the way. Our surrogate is five months, and I just thought you should know that our baby is healthy."

"Five. Months," I mouthed, squeezing my temples and taking deep breaths to control myself. This shit was making my head spin.

"Are you ready to be an evil stepmom?" Holly asked Dayton. "Our beautiful baby will be here in a little less than four months. And if you know anything about Atlas, he's not going to turn his back on family, especially not the child he's always wanted."

"You are one sick bitch. You don't see anything wrong with what you've done, do you?" Dayton asked her.

Holly had the nerve to shake her head with a smirk on her face.

"I'm giving my husband the child he's always wanted. I'm a little late, but it's the least I can do."

"Ex husband," I bit out, lifting a stiff finger and taking a step closer that forced Holly to take a cautious step back. I would never lay a hand on any woman, but it didn't stop me from wishing I could strangle this one.

"Get out of my house right now. I can't stand to see you anymore," I forced the words out through gritted teeth. Anger pushed through me so hard that I couldn't think straight and was forced to slam my eyes shut to block Holly from my view. Deep breaths weren't the healing balm they usually were to me. Not this time. Not with this woman.

"I'll come back when you're in a better mood so we can have a private conversation about our child," she said before dropping her gaze to my dick area. "You did just come, so you should be a lot calmer unless your little redbone side piece has trash pussy and can't make you come like I can."

"You straight-out-the-psych-ward hoe," Dayton said, taking a step toward Holly while aiming a stiff finger at her. I caught Dayton around the waist and noticed Holly had enough common sense left to step back.

"I'll come back when you're in a better mood," she told me, grinning before she walked out of my kitchen.

I gripped my forehead and squeezed—my other arm still wrapped tight around Dayton's waist.

"And I thought I had a fucked-up life. That shit was straight-up psycho. And she was dead ass serious, wasn't she?" Dayton asked.

I nodded.

"This is the kind of shit she pulled our entire marriage. I swear she wasn't that damn crazy when my parents introduced me to her."

Dayton shook her head. "Yes, she was that crazy. You don't get to that level overnight. She knew how to hide that shit long enough until she had you by the balls. How the hell are you going to handle this situation? She impregnated someone with your child almost three years after your divorce?"

My head was pounding. I needed a stiff drink.

"I don't know what the fuck I'm going to do."

Chapter Fourteen

Atlas

There wasn't a mental health specialist in the world who could make me understand my ex-wife. The woman was nuts. Never in a million years would I have believed I would become a father this way.

In a few days, I was meeting the surrogate, who likely assumed I was an asshole for allowing my *wife* to do this alone. I'm sure that was the story Holly had fed the woman.

It was unfair for Dayton to be dragged into the mess that swirled around what was supposed to be my normal life.

I didn't know how to feel about the situation anymore.

Did I want to be a father? Yes, I absolutely wanted the honor. Did I want my child's mother to be Holly? Absolutely not.

On one hand, becoming a father had always been one of my dreams. I wanted to be for my child what my parents failed to be for me: caring, supporting, teaching, understanding, nourishing, and loving them unconditionally.

How the hell was I going to make any of my life as a parent work with an ex-wife I wanted to have committed and a girlfriend I adored more than anything?

Despite all the chaos swirling in my own life, I still had to find time to assist Trent with a major problem in his, as he believed his girlfriend's ex-boyfriend was stalking them.

I used a few of my resources to gather information on Donni Lorenz Armstrong. Based on what I knew about the man, including the knowledge of him drugging Callie, I agreed that he was who was stalking Trent and Callie.

After playing the part of detectives, staking out his house, and spying on him about an hour ago, we discovered that Donni was carrying drugs. We believed his intentions were to drug another woman, which led us to this club we had tailed him to so we could enact our plan of catching him in the act. We prayed the hardcore evidence would send him to jail where he belonged.

"There goes that motherfucker again. And he's with Callie's friend, Dayton," I pointed Donni out, cursing because I had to pretend Dayton and I weren't dating, as per her request. Trent and Ransome didn't know how I felt about Dayton, but they were going to find out because seeing her with someone else had me about to commit murder.

I bit deep enough into my lip to taste blood, my eyes zeroing in on Donni standing way too close to Dayton. I didn't care if we weren't an official couple. If he laid a hand on her, it was over.

"Callie's friend is an asshole for messing with her friend's ex, but we can't let him drug her. She has no idea the kind of snake that sick fuck is," Trent gritted out, his gaze deadly enough to be declared a weapon.

Seeing Dayton cozying up to that sick fuck lit my fuel-soaked blood. I had to find calm, or I was about to be paying for this club after I ripped it to shreds along with Donni. This was just what I needed to add to my pile of drama. The woman I wanted, the one I couldn't stop thinking about, was running around with the woman-drugging ex-boyfriend of her best friend.

"I'll run interference," I volunteered and stormed off before Ransome or Trent could stop me. I was a ticking time bomb, waiting for the right word, a hand gesture, a facial twitch, anything that would allow me to pound out my anger. And Donni-the-douchebag was the perfect target.

I ignored him and walked into Dayton's path to prevent her from going any farther with that asshole. Callie had to have warned Dayton about Donni drugging her. Therefore, the six-million-dollar question of the night was, *What the hell was Dayton doing with Donni's slimy ass?*

The frown on her face would have made a lesser man shrink into the floor, but I smiled at her like we were out on another date. Neither of us said a word, but our stares were holding a conversation that we couldn't keep up with, let alone decipher.

"Excuse me," Donni glanced across Dayton's shoulder at me before he took a possessive step closer and lifted a questioning palm.

"Don't you see me standing here?"

I didn't acknowledge that the asshole had even spoken. Instead, I kept my gaze pinned on Dayton's. I know she saw the question in my eyes and should have sensed the anger radiating off my edgy body.

What the hell are you doing in this club with him?

My head tilted at her non-verbal response and odd facial expression, to my silent question.

What was she doing with her face and eyes? Her eyes darted to the left with quick flicks in Donni's direction. He couldn't see her from his position behind her, over her right shoulder.

I squinted, attempting to discern the gestures she continued to make while the asshole behind her pinned his furious stare on me. He reached past Dayton and waved a hand in front of my face.

"Hey, dumb ass, don't you see me standing here? She's with me, doesn't know you, and is clearly not interested. Now, beat it."

My gaze lifted from Dayton's, and I fixed it on Donni. I allowed him to see every bit of the pent-up rage I was ready to unleash on his ass. The idea of pissing him off even further crossed my mind. I fought a smile before I continued to ignore him, returning my attention to where it belonged.

In my peripheral, I noticed Donni glancing around the club to determine if I had brushed him off again. I reached out and took Dayton's hand, holding it longer than was appropriate for two people who weren't supposed to know each other.

I lifted our hands, edging hers closer to my lips. When she didn't pull away, I proceeded with the action until my lips brushed the back of her warm, soft skin. Our eyes remained locked on each other's, and at this moment, nothing else mattered.

Dayton lifted a dramatic eyebrow, her gaze deadlocked on my lips on the back of her hand. The smile in her eyes told me all I needed to know about my actions and how she received them.

Why was she here, at this club, in the middle of our sting operation? She and her friends were supposed to be home, having their girls' night. At least, that's what Callie had told Trent earlier tonight.

Donni seethed while watching us, his body buzzing with anger. I didn't have to see them to know that other eyes were watching this dramatic display. Was it dominance? Was it me claiming the woman I wanted and her clearly allowing me to display the claim to everyone in the building?

Chest pumping hard and fast, Donni struggled to contain his rage at this public display of disrespect.

"I don't see a ring on her finger, and I'm talking to *her*, not you," I finally addressed him. He'd allowed me to see how bruised his ego was at my disrespect.

When my bold gaze lifted and finally met Donni's red-hot one again, the tension in the room grew thick enough to choke us all.

"It's not that serious," Dayton muttered to break up the friction. She was doing something funny with her eyes again.

An annoying amount of huffing, puffing, and muttering came from Donni before he shot daggers at Dayton for not sending me away.

I was coiled tight enough to snap, roaring with a fiery tension, all aimed at Donni. The one to break the standoff that would end in one of us bleeding was me, spotting Ransome and Trent approaching out of the corner of my eye.

I bent, leaning in so I could whisper in Dayton's ear. This additional display of disrespect to Donni was all he could take. He shoved me hard.

Trent and Ransome were rushing to my side within seconds.

"Is everything all right here?" Trent asked, walking up and standing beside me with his fists balled up tightly at his sides. Ransome walked up next, calling Donni's attention. He didn't know which of us to look at, so his eyes bounced over Trent, Ransome, and me.

My erratic breathing, coiled body, and flared nostrils did nothing to alleviate the pressure of my anger. Dayton was looking at me like she'd never seen me before, her head eased back, her gaze cocked and scanning me.

Donni aimed a stiff, angry finger in my direction, but his eyes were on Ransome.

"Your disrespectful-ass friend doesn't know how to take a hint. She doesn't want him," Donni said, using his head as a pointer between Dayton and me. Now, that's where he was wrong. He couldn't accept the fact that she had disrespected him as much as I had when she allowed me to kiss her hand and whisper in her ear.

Donni's forehead creased with tension, and his gaze became fixed with a knowing glint. It was no longer me or Ransome who bore the weight of his rage.

"You," he gritted out, his anger boiling over and aimed at Trent now that he recognized him.

"All my friend here is trying to do is protect this woman from a predator like you," Trent stated through clenched teeth, fighting to contain his own flaring rage. Donni was toxic. With just one look at him, my desire to punch him in the face grew so intense it became difficult to control the urge.

"Trent." Callie walked up to us and squeezed her body between mine and Trent's so she was now standing beside him. Her presence did nothing more than add fuel to this already out-of-control fire. Donni's gaze bounced back and forth between her and Trent.

"Callie. You don't have to lower your standards and settle for this loser. Come back to me, baby, and we can talk about things," he said.

When Donni reached for Callie, all our eyes landed on his hand, and our bodies automatically leaned protectively over hers. The glares we aimed at Donni were deadly enough to cause physical damage. Callie ignored his hand, forcing him to drop it.

"We can work things out," he continued like he wasn't surrounded by a group of ravenous sharks ready to rip him to pieces.

"Who the fuck are you calling a loser, you fucking sex-stealing freak?" Trent spat, jumping in his face so fast it took Ransome and me to snatch him back.

Donni grinned at the display, unbothered. He gazed back at Callie, even as we held Trent back.

"Like I was saying, baby…"

He reached up and suggestively stroked Callie's shoulder. All I wanted to do was let Trent go, but my big brother mentality kicked in, and I gripped him tighter.

"Leave that fucking broke-ass joke alone and come back to me." The man didn't know when to stop. Trent charged at him again, only to drag us about a foot as we fought to hold him back. Donni wanted a fight. I was sure of it. We needed to get Trent away from him before this train wreck drove even further off the rails.

Donni lifted his hand and made a circling motion, and his men came from the crowd. At least six of them approached us. A few stood behind him like good little guard dogs while a few remained in the distance, waiting and watching.

"Take a look around before you leap, frog. Wouldn't want you to end up…well, you know," he threatened Trent before glancing up and putting his eyes on Ransome and me.

"You think I care about how many men you've hired to fight for you? I'll still mop this floor with your ass," Trent yelled.

"I wish you would lay a hand on me. I'll fuck up your world so bad, you'll beg rock-bottom to take you back," Donni spat at Trent with that condescending grin that irked my nerves.

Knowing the move would send Trent even further over the edge, Donni reached down and ran his hand along Callie's arm, touching her again. She jerked away.

"Don't you touch her, you fucking lunatic!" Trent yelled out.

Callie turned to Trent, placing a delicate hand against his chest.

"Let's go, baby," Callie said, waiting for Trent to acknowledge her. Trent glanced down, and I could literally see some of his anger melt away. The power of a good woman. I'd seen it before, but not this close-up.

"Callie, don't be a fucking fool. You're too good for him. He can't elevate you. He's only going to use you to make a come-up. He's nothing but poor, white, drug-addicted trash."

Each word landed a physical punch to Trent's jaw.

I loosened my hold on Trent. Enough was enough. I had the means to get us out of jail if it came to that. Ransome must have gotten the memo, or his rage had taken control of his mind like mine.

Trent scooted Callie to the side, and I did the same with Dayton before Trent took an angry step closer to Donni.

"You motherfucker!" Trent barked right before he threw a punch that missed Donni's face by a millimeter. I didn't have time to process all that was happening in the few seconds that Trent had been released because an explosion erupted in my jaw.

The hard punch intensified my need to expel my anger, and I took it out on the guy who'd hit me. His next blow struck empty space, but my uppercut caught him under the chin before my right hook met his jaw with a hard head-snapping punch that had him staggering away from me.

I dodged another fist and spun to give myself enough momentum to send a combination of punches at another of Donni's goons.

Even in the midst of the fighting, one thought stuck in my head: this night wasn't going the way we'd planned. It damn sure wasn't going the way I'd pictured it in my head. I'd envisioned it ending with Donni going to jail to allow me the time I needed to pour my energy and attention into Dayton.

Chapter Fifteen

Dayton

After the shit show at the club, we, men and women, agreed to link back up at Trent's house. Discovering that the men had been at the club for the same reason as us was a pleasant surprise. I respected them for stepping up where the authorities had failed.

They voiced their concerns for our safety enough times for me to know that they didn't like the idea of us *women* putting ourselves in jeopardy to catch Donni slipping. It was too damn bad that both our sting operations were botched. Donni was probably someplace laughing at us while we were gathered in Trent's living room attempting to iron out a plan to catch him.

Atlas and I were casual friends with benefits. At least, that's what I labeled us. He'd made it clear that he wanted more, but I was still on the fence. It was why I had asked him not to mention us. I believe my request hurt his ego, but he respected my wishes, and we avoided each other as much as possible.

However, when it was time to leave Trent's, it didn't stop Atlas from asking me if I would like to join him for a drink. He'd slipped the address to where he wanted me to meet him into my pocket before walking off.

Now, I was driving around with a frown on my face. Where the hell was this man leading me to, *the promised land?*

The thought brought on an instant smile. He was not just good in bed—he was the best I'd ever been with and had left no need unsatisfied.

I eased my foot off the gas and glanced around when the GPS led me into a residential neighborhood. Had his slick ass given me the address to his house instead of the bar I was expecting to see? It was exactly what he'd done, judging by the way these houses kept getting more expensive and bigger the further I drove.

Now, here I was, sitting in the driveway of his two-story stone and brick mansion, trying to figure out if I wanted to go inside. Doing so would only lead to us fucking. He knew it, and I damn sure knew it.

Fucking was a good thing, I decided, slinging my door open and climbing out. Fucking didn't mean a relationship. Fucking didn't mean having to worry about each other's feelings. Fucking wasn't a commitment. Fucking didn't tag him as my man or me as his woman.

The large glass and wood-framed door was pushed open before I stepped into the entryway.

"I'm glad you decided to stop by," he had the nerve to say like I was paying him a casual visit.

"Um, hum," I said, walking past him and entering the house.

The first sight of the inside knocked the air clean out of my lungs. Crown molding, tall ceilings, and large floor-to-ceiling windows. There was a skylight that opened over a large portion of the living room. I was gawking so hard that I noticed the skylight had a feature that would allow it to be opened and closed like a sunroof.

Every eye movement was snagged by another beautiful feature: shiny marble floors, expensive art on the walls, sculptures of beautiful objects I couldn't name, as well as immaculately made art pieces displayed in strategic locations throughout the space. A wall of stone cladding highlighted an oversized fireplace. The list of amenities stretched on to infinity.

"I'll give you a tour if you'd like. But, first, I'll make us some drinks."

"No," I said way louder than I intended. "There is no need for a tour. You and I both know why I'm here, so let's not play house. A drink would be nice, though. I'll take something strong."

He nodded, and I didn't miss the disappointment my words left dancing in his gaze. He turned and walked across the room to a full-sized bar. He stepped behind a bar area and began mixing us some drinks. I ambled closer and sat on one of the barstools.

This area, although off the living room, made it feel like I was inside an authentic bar. The setup was impeccable and impressive.

Atlas handed me a drink, allowing his fingers to brush my hand on purpose. The warmth of his touch and the coldness of the glass felt good, sparking within me a jolt of awareness I didn't know I was suppressing.

I took the first sip of my drink after watching him take his second.

"Mm. That's good," I complimented.

His brows knitted. "Aren't you going to ask what it is?"

I shrugged. "Does it matter? Besides, I saw you pour a generous amount of vodka into these glasses along with some sort of juice to cut it."

He leaned over the bar, getting closer to me. I didn't back off, enjoying our proximity more than I cared to admit. I took a long look around the area, distracting myself.

"Do you live here by yourself?" I asked.

"Yes. It's just me. I have someone come in a few times a week and clean, and another comes in and cooks for me a few days a week as well. I spend more time at work than here, and that's the reason I also have the penthouse."

I nodded. I'd never been this up close and personal with anyone with his level of wealth. Hearing him talk about it didn't make it feel real.

"You don't act uppity or like any of the other rich pricks I've met before. You don't act like someone who has maids and cooks."

His face creased into a tight knot.

"How do I act?"

I pursed my lips, wanting to voice a smart comment, but decided to go with the truth.

"You're normal. You don't have that asshole attitude that some rich people carry around like a purse or wallet. Some take the term privilege to a whole new level. I've witnessed some of them behave like the rest of the world was their help."

He shook his head, his smile sad. He knew what I was talking about.

"All it takes sometimes is for them to truly experience what it would be like to be stripped of their power, their privilege, and control of the outcome of their own lives," he said.

I stared at him, taking a long swig of my drink. There was a lot more to him than met the eyes.

"And you've experienced being powerless, stripped of your privilege, or without control over your life?"

He nodded.

"All three."

My face crinkled. "What happened to you that would allow all three of those experiences to impact your life?" I asked.

Would he tell me? I hadn't come here for anything other than a drink and some sex, but Atlas was quickly becoming more interesting than my lust-fueled desires.

"At age eleven, I was taken for ransom," he stated. This snatched my attention. "They would beat me for the hell of it, starve me, and lock me inside this casket they had in their basement for long stretches of time. They would leave me inside until I would panic so hard I would hurt myself trying to get out."

He spoke about it casually, like he was talking about someone else. Maybe it was the way he dealt with what happened to him.

"During that time, I experienced degradation on every level. I was powerless to stop them from beating me. I had no control over when I ate, slept, talked, or even moved. I was stripped bare of any semblance of the privileged life I had lived up until my captivity. Even the chance of being rescued was chased away, burned in the flames of their hate. I was unable to fight for myself, plead my case, or find a way to free myself. I was at their mercy, only given what they believed I deserved."

I swallowed hard. It sounded like what many Black Americans attempted to get closed-minded people in this country to understand. Some don't want to understand that many of us aren't poor by choice but more so due to a system designed only to offer us scraps by way of opportunity. There was no generational wealth accumulated when most of our ancestors worked for free.

Stop, I demanded of myself. I had to cut this line of thinking short before I started preaching. This wasn't the time, and I got the sense that Atlas had educated himself and was acutely aware of the other side of history.

He took down the rest of his drink in one long swig.

"I didn't mean to stir the conversation into a subject matter that's going to bring you down. Are you okay? Going through something like that must have left a lasting impression on you."

I placed a caring hand on his forearm.

He pinned on a smile.

"I'm okay with talking about it. I just realized what matters to me most is what you asked me."

I lifted a brow, not following him.

"You asked me if I was okay?" he pointed out.

I still wasn't getting his drift. Wasn't that what you asked people when they have suffered through trauma, and you recognized the lasting effect of their suffering? The grief of that event seeped out of Atlas's pores, shone through his gaze, and peeked through his facial expressions as tiny twitches. There was no way he was okay.

"My parents never asked me that question before. Come to think of it, neither did my ex-wife. No one in my family asked me if I was okay?"

My lips fell apart at the revelation.

"My parents told me the experience made me stronger. They naturally assumed that I was strong enough to deal with it, even with the nightmares, lashing out at other kids, even cursing my parents out. They tossed me to a therapist and told them to fix me," he said, and I didn't miss the glint of hurt in his eyes.

I shook my head, my lips parted.

"That's all kinds of fucked up. This shit is pissing me off. Makes me want to give your parents a piece of my mind."

My rant had him grinning, and I didn't know why until I noticed my own agitation. The idea of him being so blatantly disregarded made me protective of him and his feelings. He stared at me for a long time before he spoke.

"Another drink?" he asked, shaking the ice at the bottom of his glass while watching me gulp down the last of my drink.

"Don't mind if I do," I said, handing him my glass back.

The sound of him pouring and mixing our drinks was all that kept the silence spilling into the room at bay.

Instead of handing me my drink over the bar like he did the first time, he walked around it and stood before me on the bar stool.

"Let's sit on the couch and get more comfortable," he suggested.

I nodded before hopping down and following him. The first drink had mellowed me out. Thankfully, I didn't have to work the next day.

Atlas waited until I was seated before handing me my drink and sitting next to me. He allowed his leg to brush mine, the contact giving off a more relaxing charge than a sexual one.

"Were the bad guys ever caught? Sometimes it's good to have someone more personal than a doctor to talk to about that type of trauma," I said, jumping right back into our conversation, interested in more details of his abduction.

He reared back, showing me a wide-eyed expression that said my question and statement were unexpected.

"Please don't be offended by this, but you're always so tough and to the point. I didn't believe you'd want to hear about me and my childhood trauma," he told me.

"Have you ever heard the saying, don't judge a book by its cover? Well, don't judge this book by its loud-mouth. Do you think I would have friends like Callie and Charlene if I were half as bad as my mouth suggests I am?" I said, laughing at my own silly statement. Atlas grinned along with me. His eyes filled with an emotion I couldn't pinpoint.

"There's not much more to tell. I suffered at the hands of my kidnappers for a month before they decided to let me go. My parents had gotten law enforcement involved. It took some time, a little over three years of investigations and me reliving the nightmare through questions from the cops for them to finally find leads. The group ended up being a group of white nationalists who specifically targeted wealthy families that held opposing views on life, politics, and even religion. They would go around kidnapping the kids for ransom to fund their causes, most of them having racist ideologies."

That's why he was so down to earth. As bad as it sounded, even in my head, sometimes it took a tragic wake-up call to get people to open their eyes and minds. When you opened your mind and began to see the world for what it truly was, others no longer had the ability to paint you the picture of it that they wanted you to see.

"When all was said and done, the authorities discovered that fifteen other kids that they knew about had been kidnapped and over ten million dollars in payouts had been given to the group. Although they hadn't given themselves an official name, there were over a hundred members in four states. When they held me, they treated me like I was the scum of the earth because my family didn't support their views and was known to campaign and fight against groups like theirs."

I shook my head at the incredible story. It was hitting home for me in a roundabout way that I understood too well.

"Most of the group was arrested and thrown into jail."

I held my glass up, sending a toast in his direction for having survived such a tragic event and not receiving any real emotional support after it was over.

"I would still like to give your parents a good talking to. However, there is one thing I have to agree with them on. That ordeal has made you a stronger man, especially your mental strength," I complimented.

He leaned into me after the statement, bumping his shoulder against mine. My smile surfaced when he didn't pull away, leaving me to bask in the inviting warmth flowing from him.

We sipped our drinks in silence, allowing the cold liquid to mellow us down to drooping eyes and shoulders. This wasn't the hot butt-naked sex I'd anticipated, but in a weird way, it was better.

Chapter Sixteen

Dayton

"What about you, Dayton?"

The question threw me off after such a long and oddly comfortable silence had fallen between us.

"You don't gain the kind of strength you carry around without training or grooming. The night I walked into that hotel room and saw you facing off with a man who towered a foot over you, I honestly didn't know whether to be afraid for him or you," he stated.

I grinned, my shoulders shaking at the idea.

"Assholes like him are why I would risk it all to help someone who doesn't know how or can't fight for themselves. He's the kind of man who deserves a hot pot of grits thrown on him."

"Ouch. That sounds like torture."

I nodded because it was torture, and I had slung grits on a man before in my lifetime.

"Imagine spending years with a man who would lay hands on you at the drop of a dime and sometimes for no other reason than to remind you that he has the upper hand. Imagine being raped repeatedly by the person you married, and you can't report it or say anything because, in society's eyes, you're husband and wife, and it doesn't count as rape. I've seen it all and then some," I stated.

I allowed the silence to linger because the subject always pissed me off.

"Aren't you afraid that one day, things could go too far, and they could hurt you or kill you when all you're there to do is help?" he questioned, and I could hear his concern for me in his tone.

I nodded. "Of course I'm afraid, but my fear gets overshadowed by my will to end a woman's suffering. To know that my help, no matter how big or small, can stop a murder or put an end to months or years of abuse. Do you know how many domestic abuse cases end in murder when the abuser goes too far and kills, or the abused gets pushed too far and kills?"

He tilted his head at the impacting words, absorbing them.

"I can imagine that it never ends well when it does. Were you ever in a domestic abuse situation? Is that why you fight for women so profoundly?"

I swallowed hard. It was hard to explain why I chose to fight when I could just as well let the authorities handle it.

"You've seen me naked. You know that I tan. All my young life, I was picked on for being light-skinned. My mother was a few shades darker than me, and my father has a deep brown tone. So, imagine my light complexion being presented to my father after my mother had given him three brown sons. I had a DNA test done when I was a baby and one later when I was a young girl. Apparently, even after years of knowing I was his biological daughter, my father had to have a reminder."

I paused and took a breather because my family drama wasn't something I liked talking about to anyone.

"Since almost everyone in my family is brown or darker, they often teased me for being lighter, claiming that I thought I was better than them. Imagine hearing this your whole young life, that your own family didn't like you because your skin was a different shade. And despite two DNA tests, most of my family still tells my father that I'm not his child. Therefore, I've been fighting for myself against my own family since before I even understood what I was doing. It also didn't help matters that my mother was a cheat. Half the town knew she ran around on my father. It was one of her side boyfriends who beat and killed her because she'd refused to leave my father for him when I was seven. Despite the trouble between my parents, I loved my mother. She was a good mother. Her death is what also drives me to fight for women, to keep them from losing their lives to an abusive man."

A glance at Atlas showed me a deer-in-the-headlights look before he gulped down a hard swallow. He wanted to know my story, and this liquor had loosened up my tongue.

"Fast forward: no mother, being raised up by a father who had doubts about me being his daughter, and three older brothers who picked on me for being lighter. My young life was filled with insults and tough love. I had no choice but to be strong. I discovered at nine that if I played in the sun, it made my skin darker, like my father's and brothers'. So, the sun became my best friend."

Atlas remained silent, my words making him shake his head and lift his brows.

"The jabs about my complexion still came after I found a way to temporarily darken myself, but not nearly as often as before. If something good happened to me: honor roll, winning a school contest, or being picked for sports or clubs, I never got the proud embrace that the other kids received for achieving. I received comments like, "You only won that because of your light skin and your good hair. You only got into that club because you passed the paper bag challenge. The shit did a number on my young mind. I started tanning when I was fourteen. I still do now, but not as much as I did when I was younger."

The horrified look on Atlas's face expressed more than he was clearly capable of saying right now. Now that he had me spilling my guts, I couldn't stop the well of raw emotions from flowing free.

"It's taken years, but I've finally convinced my father and brothers to attend a few therapy sessions with me. I'm hoping it will at least allow them to see how much the way they view me hurts."

He nodded, the sincerity in his gaze not missed.

"You think you can stand one more drink, or have you had enough?" Atlas asked when silence lingered too long.

"One more," I told him, handing him the glass and realizing I had emptied the glass of even the ice.

I rarely talked about my childhood, even with my best friends, but for reasons I couldn't pinpoint, it was easy to spill my guts to Atlas. Maybe it was because he'd told me about his childhood trauma and the way his parents had brushed it off.

I stood, and when my body didn't do the shaky wave it did to let me know it was time to cut the drinks off, I smiled.

"Will you point me to the bathroom?" I asked Atlas. He lifted the glass of ice in his hand, pointing me in the direction of a staircase that belonged in a magazine. I ambled in that direction until I found the first door I could open and stepped inside.

After using the bathroom and washing my hands, I glanced in the mirror at myself, staring at my reflection. This night wasn't going the way I had envisioned it, but I wasn't disappointed. It felt good to get some of the things I keep bottled up inside, out of my system.

A glance at my watch showed me it was verging into the next day at 3:12 a.m. Damn, it didn't feel that late in the morning. I aimed a finger at my reflection.

"Have that last drink and take your tired ass home," I warned myself out loud.

I walked back and eased up beside Atlas, who had his head thrown back on the couch. His eyes snapped open, and a wide grin spread across his face before I could take my seat.

He watched me sit. There was an emotion in his eyes like earlier that I couldn't place. He leaned over and picked up our drinks from the coffee table before handing me mine.

"Was this your plan? To get me to your house, get me drunk, and have hot naked sex with me?"

He shook his head after sitting his drink down.

"Believe it or not, I just wanted to see you—wanted your company. My everyday life is such a mess of drama that it's nice to be around someone who I can be myself with and not have to worry about a whole lot of crazy," he said.

"I chase down abusive men and threaten to kick their asses in my spare time. You don't consider that drama?"

He laughed.

"When you put it that way, it does sound dramatic and problematic, but you're helping people. What you're doing is admirable. It's not a petty kind of drama that's designed to cause chaos."

I sipped and sat still, feeling the cool liquid travel all the way down until it warmed my belly.

"Would you like to finish telling me about your childhood?" he asked. He hadn't lost his interest in my story.

I glanced at him, my forehead creased.

"What makes you think that there's more to tell?"

He shrugged. "I sensed that there was more, and I'm aware that it must be difficult to talk about the biases you faced from society and even more so at the hands of your own family.

He was right and a lot more perceptive than I gave him credit for. I believe he was also open-minded enough to understand and appreciate my reality, the way I lived it as a woman and a woman of color.

Did I want to open the box of emotions that I had double-locked in my head?

"It's okay. You can talk to me anytime, by phone or in person, and I promise you, I'll make time for you," he said, his words sounding genuine.

This got a side-eye out of me. Was he...

"Yes, I'm serious. I like you, Dayton. A lot. The things I never truly got out of the people in my life are the things that I am mindful of: time, understanding, and communication. I couldn't get my ex-wife to comprehend this, but that's okay. It took me a while to accept that she was never my person."

My forehead wrinkled into a tight knot.

"And you believe that I am?"

He nodded.

"I know it may sound like I'm being presumptuous and assuming, but yes, I do."

Since the day I met this man, he'd been adamant that I was the woman for him.

"What do you see in me that would make you know that I'm your person?" I asked, wanting to know.

He inhaled deeply before releasing.

"It's more a feeling than something I see. Am I attracted to you? Beyond what's probably appropriate to say. Do I want to have a lot of sex with you? In every imaginable way. But it's more than the physical aspects that draw me to you. Something within you speaks to me on a level I don't understand but know I should cling to desperately."

I didn't know what else to say. My quick-tongued, big-mouthed self didn't have a response. No one had ever laid out how they felt or connected with me on that level. His response floored me. It made me acknowledge that the connection he couldn't properly describe also lingered within me. Unlike him, I'd been doing my best to ignore it, hoping the lingering sensation would disappear. Maybe sex would make it go away.

We allowed silence to consume us after I didn't respond to his statement. My head fell to his shoulder, and his warm strength relaxed me. Minutes passed until I jerked my bobbing head up. Atlas smiled. He'd been watching me nod off.

He reached down, lifted my legs, and dragged them across his thighs before taking off my heels. He moved a pillow from his side of the couch and placed it behind me. The next thing I knew, one of my feet was in his strong hands. I fell back on the pillow and released a deep sigh at him massaging the soreness in my feet away.

This felt like a moment of perfection I wouldn't have minded being trapped in. Atlas was determined to grow on me, and I wondered for the first time since we initiated this unofficial relationship if I might give him a chance.

Chapter Seventeen

Atlas

Dayton's ringing phone pulled us both out of a deep sleep. She hopped up, glanced down at the way we had been laid out on my couch together, reached onto the coffee table, and snatched it up all before the ringtone sounded a second time.

"Hello."

I don't know what was being said on the other end of the line, but her expression, one dripping fear, said enough for me to be concerned.

"What? Wait. Slow down. Did you say Trent's been shot?"

Holy shit!

I jumped up off the couch, already searching for keys and my phone, although I didn't know the full story.

Keys in hand, shoes on, I stared at Dayton's distressed posture while she listened to what was being said on the other end of the line. I was ready to go. Where? I had no clue.

"Callie! Callie! Are you okay? What the fuck is happening?"

Dayton continued to yell, attempting to get the story out of Callie, who must have been distraught.

"Is he alive? Is he at the hospital?" I asked Dayton, hoping she could tell me something other than he'd been shot.

"I don't know. It sounds like she's talking to the cops," Dayton replied. "From what I can hear, I think paramedics are working on him."

I dialed Ransome. "Have you heard from Trent," I asked him as soon as his phone clicked on.

"No," he answered groggily.

"I think he's been shot. Dayton is on the phone with Callie right now."

"Shit. Is he okay?" Ransome asked.

I shrugged. "I don't know. Dayton's trying to…"

"Fuck!" Dayton shouted. "Is he…"

At this point, my heart was hanging from my chest, waiting for me to pick it up off the floor. Trent was the younger brother I never had, and if someone messed with him, they would have to deal with me.

Dayton clicked off. "He's been shot in the chest. It happened in his own driveway. Callie is going to text me the address to the hospital they are taking him to," she spat while slipping on her shoes.

My teeth dipped deeply into my lip, contemplating my next move until Ransome's voice sounded over the line. I returned the phone to my ear to relay the update to him.

"He's been shot in the chest. At his house. Callie is texting us the address."

"Considering the proximity to his neighborhood, they are likely going to take him to Westmore Memorial," Ransome surmised.

"Okay, I'm heading over there now. I'll text you if it's a different location," I told Ransome before clicking off.

***

Dayton

I hated hospitals. Driving up to this one made my back itch and my nerves twitch. After Atlas parked in the garage about a half mile away from the place, he and I trekked over to the main building.

It took more time to travel the corridors and hallways in three different directions to find the waiting area, where we finally spotted Callie.

Poor thing, even from a distance, I could tell she'd been crying and now was gnawing at her nails like they were hard candy.

"Callie," I called out to her so as not to scare her since her unfocused gaze made it look like she was mentally on another planet. She turned at the sound of her name and cast a quick glance at Atlas walking next to me before her troubled gaze shot over my shoulder. A glance back showed Ransome and Charlene hot on our trail and entering the waiting area as well.

"How is he?" I asked her.

Callie answered with a shoulder shrug and a sob before she relayed the details about a collapsed lung and blood in his chest cavity that left us all speechless.

Donni had to have been behind this incident. Who else would target Trent in his own front yard?

We had to make sure Trent would be okay before finding a way to put an end to this Donni character once and for all. He was irritating and relentless, like one of those biting gnats. How do you take someone like that down without doing something that would land you in jail?

"I'll go and get us some coffee," Atlas volunteered, breaking into the stiff silence that filled the room while waiting for Trent to get out of surgery.

Although Atlas and I had arrived together, I noticed that I still managed to put some space between us while we waited.

Why?

Why didn't I want anyone to know we were seeing each other? It was a question I couldn't answer.

Time ticked on like it was a member of our group. I couldn't recall if it were ten minutes, twenty, or thirty, but we all sat higher in our chairs at the doctor's approach, while collectively holding our breaths.

The doctor stood before our group, staring with his hands cupped in front of him.

Did he plan to speak or continue to stand there looking at us?

"Mr. Pierce is in recovery. The bullet was removed successfully."

Collective sighs of relief and words of thanks and gratitude were expressed while the stress of the doctor's continuing announcement kept our eyes glued to his mouth.

I hardly heard a thing the doctor said afterward. If Trent was okay, it meant Callie would be okay, too. The knowledge alone was enough to ease my troubled mind.

We hung out for another hour, drinking coffee and sneaking in one-by-one to get a quick visit with Trent. Although heavily sedated, seeing him settled our rattled nerves and provided the relief and permission we needed to finally leave the hospital.

We were becoming a close-knit group. Callie, Dayton, and I had extended invitations to allow Trent, Ransome, and Atlas into our lives whether we were ready for it or not.

"Are you ready?" Atlas asked.

He'd waited until it was just us left in the waiting room before he posed the question. As far as I knew, no one had noticed that we had arrived together, and if they did, they hadn't pointed it out. All I wanted now was to retrieve my car and go home to a long hot shower and my bed.

Chapter Eighteen

Dayton

The next day.

The drama going on with our friends had temporarily taken my and Atlas's minds off the trouble swirling around us and happening before we could officially call ourselves an *us*.

Did I want there to be an us? It had been a long time since I'd been in or even considered a relationship. I wasn't sure I knew how to be in one.

After calling in sick to work and sleeping the rest of the morning away, I finally rolled out of bed at 2 p.m. to make myself breakfast. It wasn't lost on me that the first thing I thought of when I opened my eyes was Atlas and not Callie or even Trent. I let the idea linger right where it would remain—in the back of my mind.

Music blasted, and I danced to the beat while cooking. I didn't hear a word of the song because my mind was preoccupied, doing its own thing when all I wanted was music and food.

After leaving the hospital last night, I hadn't allowed myself to walk back into Atlas's house. I attempted to make a clean break by saying a quick goodbye, but he wasn't having it. He pulled me into a bear hug that had me giggling and returning his embrace. He had a memory like an elephant, making me promise to tell him more about my childhood and life when I felt like talking.

There wasn't much more to tell, just a lot of family drama and bullying that could mess up a young girl's mind about her self-image and the way she viewed men. I still had a long way to go, but it wasn't until I learned to love myself that I began healing from years of compacted mental programming.

Now, I needed my omelet, coffee, and a Netflix therapy session before I threw something on to go and check on Callie and Trent. Callie had texted, telling me to stay home, but what kind of friend leaves their girl alone in the hospital with her shot-up boyfriend? Not me. I didn't care if Trent was admitted for an infected toe. I would be Callie's emotional support whether he ended up with nine toes or not.

The buzz of my phone vibrating on the coffee table called my attention. My fork dropped into my plate when I noticed it was Callie calling. I tossed my plate and half-eaten food on the coffee table.

"Hello," I answered, my heart kicking up a notch while I prayed it wasn't bad news.

"Trent's missing," she said, her voice so cracked I barely made out what she'd said.

Missing?

I didn't know how to respond to that, so I scratched my head. Maybe I'd not heard her correctly.

"Are you sleep-talking or code-talking or something? What do you mean he's missing?" I asked her.

The man had one good lung. Where the hell was he going to go, and how far could he get once he left?

"The hospital is saying a transfer request was submitted, and he was removed. Now, they have no idea who took him or where they took him to," she said, her voice cracking so badly I had to replay her words in my head to decode them.

What?

I removed my phone from my ear and glanced down at it. Did I hear her correctly? Was this Callie on the other end of the phone?

"Are you telling me the hospital lost Trent?"

"Yes," she answered. "His mother's here. She's trying to find out who put in the transfer. And it's just a mess. No one knows anything."

"Okay. I'll be there shortly. We are going to find him," I reassured her.

Westmore Memorial was known for being one of the best hospitals in the city. They wouldn't let someone take a patient without proper guidelines being followed. Who takes a patient from the hospital anyway?

Donni.

The trouble-making asshole was taking shit too far if he was behind this transfer. Or was it a kidnapping?

***

Later, the same day.

Shoulders shrugged, and a few, "I don't knows," sounded throughout my living room.

Ransome had posed a question that I believed we had all asked at some point after getting escorted out of the hospital by security. All because we were demanding that they do their jobs and find Trent.

Were we loud, obnoxious assholes? We probably were, but a man was missing. And not just any man. Trent was seriously injured, which posed another set of problems.

I glanced at Trent's young-looking mother, Martina. She had threatened to burn the place to the ground if they didn't find her son. Martina was small in stature, pretty, and gave off a friendly, inviting vibe, but she wasn't playing games with anyone about her son, his well-being, or his whereabouts. I believed she would have hijacked a gas truck and torched the place, and she may return and do the job if we didn't hear something soon about them finding Trent.

Atlas had threatened them with every type of lawsuit known to man. He'd had his attorney on speaker phone so the hospital staff could hear how the place could legally be ripped apart in Latin words I couldn't understand if they didn't find Trent.

It had become clear that Trent was a well-liked man. He had friends and family who were willing to raise hell to make sure he was okay.

Callie carried her stress in her eyes, making it look like she hadn't slept in eighty-five years. When was the drama going to end?

Drinks were served, theories were tossed around, and plans were made to track down Trent on our own if need be.

Sitting around waiting for a call from the hospital and the police, who couldn't track down their own ass cracks, wasn't going to cut it. Time was the enemy in this type of situation. The TV show, *The First 48*, had made that a well-known fact.

"I'm going to go home and shower and change clothes. I'll be back later," Callie announced, glancing around the room.

"We're going with you," Charlene said before I could get a word in.

"So are we," Atlas said, with Ransome nodding in the background.

"I need to be alone for a minute. I'll be careful," she assured us.

Something was up. Callie wanted to cut out in the middle of us waiting on updates about Trent. I squinted at her in an attempt to figure out what was happening in her head. She'd been the quietest person in the room for the past hour.

"Callie, we don't know where Trent is. What if someone *took* him from that hospital? That same someone could be out there waiting to get to you," I told her. She eased back on the couch at those words.

A few minutes later, Callie stood, and all eyes landed on her.

"Don't worry. I just need to use the restroom," she announced.

Atlas had been on his phone nonstop, attempting to get leads from whoever his family was connected to in the police department. Trent's mother was also on the phone. The little bends at the corners of her lips posed a promising smile.

"It was the hospital. They say the police found a lead that they are chasing down. They will let us know what they find out," she stated.

The announcement got some cheers and a few claps out of us. The question now was, how good was their information, and was it going to lead to them finding Trent?

My brows knitted.

"Where the hell is Callie? Is she taking a shit?" I questioned.

She'd never returned from the bathroom. Instead of waiting, I went to check on her.

Knock. Knock.

"Callie, are you okay in there?"

No answer.

"Callie?"

Silence on the other side of the door made me turn the knob. The door wasn't locked, so I pushed it open and stepped inside. My eyes went from the open window and around my empty bathroom to make sure my weary eyes weren't misinterpreting this scene.

I know she didn't.

I ran back into the living room, making Charlene jerk back when I began my frantic search of the coffee table.

"What's wrong?" Charlene asked.

"My keys are missing, and guess who's not in the bathroom?"

She shook her head, not believing me. "No?"

The one-word question was amplified by Charlene's bewildered facial expression. The rest of the room went eerily silent.

"I'm going to kill her," I promised. "I'm going to kill her with my bare hands," I gritted out.

I had an idea of where Callie was headed. Going to see Donni alone wasn't the best decision she could have made when we already had one missing person on our hands.

Although we hadn't mentioned it in front of Callie, she knew we were all thinking that Donni had taken Trent from that hospital. Now, I believed she was going to confront that lunatic to see if and where he had taken Trent.

What if he drugs her and locks her in a damn dungeon or something?

Were we about to have two missing persons on our hands?

My gaze met Atlas's across the room, and his reassuring smile was just as comforting as a hug.

Chapter Nineteen

Dayton

After Atlas tracked down an address for the lead the cops had, he and Ransome decided they were going to play detective and drive to the location.

Instead of us following up on the lead, too, Charlene and I were stuck in my living room waiting for Callie while planning out how best to torture her ass for worrying us like this. I had finally called up the app to track my car and noticed that she was on her way back.

My leg bounced, and my jittery body swayed to keep anger and worry from ripping me apart. Charlene, bless her heart, remained calm enough for the both of us. Martina had decided to take a shower and attempt to get a few hours of sleep in my spare bedroom. I was sure that if she did manage to fall asleep, it would be with her phone in her hand.

My car.

I hopped off the couch and made a beeline for the door, snatching it open with a major attitude. I was pissed, but at the same time, relieved to see this damn crazy-ass woman. I held the door open while Charlene and I stared daggers at Callie as she made her approach.

Sneaking off alone to go and confront her ex was not the smartest thing she'd ever done.

She took shaky steps closer, her eyes zeroing in on the ground and her feet everywhere but at us. When she finally did glance up at us, she had the nerve to flash us those big puppy dog watery eyes, and just like that, my anger disintegrated, but I still had to let her know that she'd nearly given me a heart attack.

"Get your ass in this house and give me my damn keys," I told her, hoping she felt the anger swirling in me knock her across that hard head of hers. She reminded me of a little kid who knew they were in trouble and was feigning the strength to endure it.

Charlene aimed a finger toward the bathroom. "I need to use the bathroom," she said before she stepped off in that direction. She sure was peeing a lot. It was like her bladder couldn't take all the extra drama we'd been faced with lately.

My narrowed eyes fell on Callie, who had taken a seat on the couch.

"The police and the hospital called. They found a lead and are deploying a team to see if Trent is at the place they suspect," I told her while taking a step closer so that I stood over her.

"Atlas and Ransome found out the address somehow and are taking their asses over there. I hope they don't do something stupid and keep the police from doing their jobs."

Her mouth fell open while I jiggled the keys. I was still filled to the brim with stress over what that sicko ex-boyfriend could have done to her. Based on the way she glanced at me under her lashes without saying anything, she knew it, too.

"Charlene! Hurry up and drop that water. We gotta go!"

"Go?" Callie asked.

"Yes. Go," I told her. "You don't think we're sitting here in this house and waiting patiently, do you? I made Atlas give up that address. They've only been gone for about ten minutes. So, if Charlene ever finishes peeing, we can go and get your shot up and kidnapped, man."

My words put a tiny hint of a smile into Callie's eyes.

"I'm finished," Charlene said, stepping back into the living room and rubbing lotion into her hands.

"Let's go," I said before snatching up my wallet from the coffee table and turning and marching toward the front door.

"What about Martina?" Charlene asked while following me to the door.

"Let her sleep. We'll call her if there's good news. We don't need Rambo's little sister to go charging into this place before the cops can do their jobs."

This got a chuckle out of Callie and Charlene. "Don't think you're not going to get these words I have for you about your little field trip, Callie," I called over the top of my car.

She nodded before she climbed into the back seat. I climbed in, closed the door, and fired up the engine. Charlene rode shotgun. As soon as she climbed in and slammed her door shut, I hit reverse and turned in the seat. One eye watched my rear, and the other was aimed at Callie in the dark backseat.

"That ex-boyfriend lunatic of yours could have killed you," Charlene chimed in, sounding like me.

"What if he was the one who took Trent from that hospital? What if he wasn't the one who took Trent but hired someone else to do it for him?" I questioned.

Charlene turned around from the passenger seat to get a good look at Callie. "What were you thinking? We would have gone with you. You know we wouldn't have let you go to that psycho by yourself, right?"

For a few long seconds, Callie remained silent, I supposed, gathering her words. It may have felt like we were ganging up on her, but I also prayed she knew we meant well and wanted her safe.

"Thank you. I know you would have come with me," she finally said, her voice weak, shaky. "But Trent and I have had so much drama swirling around us lately that I didn't want you getting involved any deeper."

Charlene turned to reach through the space between the seats to take Callie's hand. I also reached back, tightening my hand around hers while maintaining a firm grip on the steering wheel.

"In the infamous words of Gee Money from New Jack City, "We all we got," I said, my tone brimming with amusement now that I knew she was okay.

"Don't ever think you have to do anything on your own. We're here for you. No matter what," Charlene added.

"Thank you. I appreciate you two more than I can say right now," she choked out.

"So, what's the verdict? What did you find out? Did Donnie take Trent?"

She shook her head. "I don't think so. I know it's stupid of me to believe a word he says, but I'm not convinced it was him who took Trent."

I rubbed the center of my forehead. If Donni didn't take Trent, then who the hell did?

Flashing lights dragged my attention away from my conflicting thoughts.

"Are we in…?"

"Sherwood Forest," Charlene answered the question I didn't finish asking.

"Is Trent supposed to be inside that cupcake shop?" Callie asked, reluctance lacing her tone. It was an unlikely scenario, but it was the address Atlas had given me. The cops hanging out near it were a clear indication that we were at the right location.

I prayed hard and repeatedly that Trent was here and alive. I'm sure I wasn't the only one in the car whose mouth hung open at the sight of a SWAT team running across the road and closing in on the cupcake shop with a battering ram. No one mentioned anything about a hostage situation in progress or that there would be SWAT teams and machine guns involved.

I slammed on the brakes when I became aware that the car was driving itself for a lost moment. We came to a screeching stop and sat watching the team of black uniformed men execute practiced marching formations before ramming the pink and blue front door of the shop open.

The team filed in through the busted-up door with guns raised. More police waited behind squad cars and barricades.

We waited. And waited. What was taking so long? The stress of wanting to know and praying for a positive outcome was killing me. I couldn't imagine what Callie was feeling.

"Is that Trent?" I asked, leaning over the steering wheel for a better view to make sure I wasn't giving out false hope.

Callie hopped out of the car and took off. I snatched my door open and took off right behind her. Charlene was hot on my trail.

"Callie, slow down!"

"Callie!" Charlene and I yelled after her. Had she forgotten that she was Black and you couldn't go running toward the police and not suffer any consequences?

"You can't just go...."

"Stop right there!" the police yelled.

Callie froze, lifting her hands at the sounds of the heavy metal clicks sounding off like musical notes being struck. I slammed into Callie's back, jostling her before I righted myself and lifted my hands. Charlene stood on the opposite side of Callie with her hands raised.

"That's my boyfriend," Callie called out, moving a careful finger to point in Trent's direction while my eyes were locked on the barrel of a high-powered gun.

Trent lifted his head. He was a pale version of death warmed over with pain leaking from every part of his body, but his eyes lit up at the sight of Callie.

"Please...let them in," he called out, his words carrying the weight of his pain.

Callie ran to him, helping him, kissing and loving on him. I released the breath I believed I'd been holding since I found out Trent was missing. Now, I could go home and sleep for a week.

Chapter Twenty

Dayton

A week later.

I didn't want to smile but found it difficult to deny a face as handsome as Atlas's. I had agreed to meet him at Peppercorn, one of my favorite restaurants. The crab, the lobster, the cheesecake—everything I sampled at the restaurant was good enough to make you want to slap someone's mother. I wasn't sure how Atlas knew this was one of my favorite restaurants, but I had no problem agreeing to the invite.

"Thank you for not holding the drama my ex-wife pulled against me."

I nodded. "The ex may have initiated the drama, but I still got a mind-blowing finish. Based on her red face, wide eyes, and open mouth, I'd say she got more than she bargained for by barging into where she knew she didn't belong."

He chuckled, his expression indicating that he was relieved that I wasn't holding his ex's questionable behavior against him.

"Was she telling the truth about the surrogate and you becoming a father?"

Dread and disappointment hung heavy in his gaze, but he nodded.

"It's all true. Since it wasn't addressed in our divorce settlement, she took advantage of it. I didn't think I needed to protect myself in that way until now."

He released a long sigh while his shoulders dropped, the pressure of this situation heavy on him.

"Even if she hadn't waited until the surrogate was past the three-month mark, with the new laws, there is nothing we can do to stop the process after the surrogate became pregnant. I believe I can file a lawsuit against Holly for medical misuse of my biological material as well as sue her for custody."

"Are you going to pursue any of those avenues?"

"I would like to sue her for everything she's got, but everything she has was received from me in the divorce settlement. Now, with a baby on the way, I have to think about their welfare, which unfortunately means Holly's too."

I shook my head. She was wrong as hell for what she was doing to him, but the way he was handling it spoke for his character and patience.

"I've also considered suing for custody based on her mental health, but if they find that she has no mental issues, she can counter-sue me. This whole situation is a bit tricky, not so much in the eyes of the law, but the tightrope I have to walk regarding what's best for the child."

I nodded. "I understand where you're coming from. But, once your son or daughter arrives, you're going to have to deal with Holly whether you want to or not."

His head moved robotically with a nod, his brows tightening before he bit into his bottom lip, thinking. "I know."

He stared across the table, his vision projecting past me for a long moment before he spoke.

"I know it's not fair to drag you into a situation like this, but I still want to be with you if you'll have me. And I promise you that I'll do everything in my power to make sure you stay clear of any of this."

His handsome face dropped at my long moment of silence. The bright spark of hope in his eyes that I had spotted a moment ago was reduced to a glimmer.

"You know I was reluctant from the beginning about starting anything with you." I paused, gathering my words. "I enjoy the peace of not having to deal with drama or worrying about someone else's feelings. I'm selfish with my time. I like fighting for other women. That's my drama, but it's the kind of drama that gives me satisfaction. I'm hesitant about placing myself in a situation where I may be forced to give up what little peace of mind I've created for myself."

He nodded, his eyes heavy, his face dropping at my words.

"I like you, Atlas. I can admit that much to myself. You're a good man. You have some admirable qualities. Some questionable ones, too. But have you asked yourself why you're pursuing me? What is it about me that resonates with you to the point of wanting a relationship?"

He glanced at me like maybe I should already know the answer.

"The first time I saw you at the club, you saw me dance, but you didn't see me after I left the stage. I watched you from afar for a short time. Our brief encounter while I was dancing created this magnetic pull toward you. When I saw your face, there was this…how can I say this without sounding crazy? There was this knowledge, something within me that felt like it knew you on a level that I didn't understand, still don't understand. When I saw you again at the restaurant that day when Ransome came to your table, and Trent and I invited ourselves over, I felt the same connection."

I didn't know how to respond to his impactful words. I would be lying if I said I didn't feel the same pull he was attempting to describe. It was new, different, and unrelenting. What did it mean? Were we supposed to be together? Were we supposed to initiate and start a relationship? I didn't know.

"Honestly, I've never had a relationship that I would call successful," I told him, making one of his eyebrows lift at the comment. "I've not wanted to try because it always feels like I'm the one losing something in the building part of it. So, I date, we have sex or not, and I move on, no strings, no hurt feelings, no drama. I've come to like it that way. However..." I paused, sweeping my scattered thoughts into a neat little pile in my head.

"I'm getting older, and I have considered what it might be like to at least try. But, I won't go for anything less than a dependable, honest, and loyal partner," I said, emphasizing those words. "I already have an unbothered attitude when it comes to relationships, so I will not tolerate games and bullshit."

Atlas remained silent, processing my words, but I noticed the spark of hope had returned to his eyes.

"I believe I owe it to myself to at least try. I can't promise you all the glitz and glam that people trick themselves into believing a relationship is supposed to be, but I'll make time to see you when I can. Talk to you if you need it. And other...things," I said, my smile showing up and adding more depth to my words.

He nodded. "It would make me happy if you tried," he said as the joy in his expression spilled over to me.

Light talk about the food and wine followed along with some of Atlas's corny jokes and my cheesy ones. The thing I enjoyed best about us was our ability to get on the same page on topics. I learned that Atlas, like me, enjoyed people-watching and analyzing them.

"What about her dress?" I asked Atlas, referring to a woman who had to have pulled the drapes off her living room windows and tossed them on before she left the house.

He didn't answer, only watched the woman with a stare as stiff as his posture as she and her date, I presumed, stepped closer.

"Do you know her?" I asked him.

"She's who my parents want me to marry. Did I tell you my parents have a penchant for pimping me out to millionaires and billionaires for business purposes? Golf games, exclusive sex clubs, dates with older, younger, sisters, wives—it doesn't matter as long as I can make them smile and, in some cases, make them happy. I'm set up to 'take one for the family' as they call it."

He most certainly had not told me about that kind of shit, although I'd picked up on hints of it when he'd told me about what happened to him when he was a child.

"Are you serious?" I asked while my gaze remained pinned on the leggy blonde walking our way. Up close, her face was pretty and would have been beautiful if not for so much makeup. However, she was model-thin and wore her privileged status like it was a shawl tossed over her shoulders.

"Atlas," she spoke when she stepped up to our table, her tone low and subdued like her personality. She ignored me— didn't even cast a fleeting glance in my direction. Atlas didn't stand to greet her but presented a nod and forced smile in her direction.

"Evangeline," he greeted.

"Aren't you going to introduce me to your friend?" she asked him, still not looking in my direction.

Be cool, I told myself.

"You first," he countered, looking at her friend or date.

"Atlas. This is Evan Sutton, my cousin from California," she introduced.

The man stuck out his hand, and the eagerness in his expression and quick body movement said he didn't share the same stuck-up personality as his cousin.

"Atlas. So nice to meet you. I've heard a lot of good things about you, and the improvements you've made with Belair Enterprises are impressive," Evan complimented.

Atlas' smile surfaced for the first time.

"Thank you. I appreciate the compliment." Atlas cleared his throat before sending a quick glance in my direction. "Evangeline, Evan, this is my girlfriend, Dayton."

It took every cell in my body not to react to him introducing me as his girlfriend. Evan stuck out his hand and shook mine. Evangeline turned her nose up before she put on the fakest smile I'd ever seen. Her attitude didn't matter to me because I didn't want to be introduced to her anyway.

"Don't let me hold you guys up," Atlas stated, off-key telling them to beat it.

"I'm going to have to postpone the investment meeting we have set up for Wednesday. My assistant will call you and let you know when it can be rescheduled," Evangeline stated snidely.

Atlas's eyes twitched, indicating his irritation, before he flashed another fake smile.

"Of course," he finally replied.

"Enjoy your dinner. It was nice meeting you, Evan," he told her cousin. This second brushoff wasn't as smooth as the first. Atlas didn't want this woman around him. Although the tension of his irritation wasn't showing on his smiling face, I sensed it.

The cousin turned and gave a little friendly wave while Evangeline stomped off toward their table.

"I'm starting to understand now why you use stripping as therapy. It looks like you've been used so much in your life that you accept a lot that many others wouldn't. And here I was thinking I had issues with my family."

"Sorry about that. My parents and her parents are the reason for that particular issue. They all but engaged me to the woman without consulting me first."

"And you don't see anything wrong with that?" I asked.

"Of course I do. And I tell them all the time. They grew up in an age and time when it was acceptable to use children, marriages, relationships, and, in some cases, sex to cut deals. I caught the tail end of their era, and although I go along with some of the crazy, I put my foot down when they take things too far."

I aimed a finger over my shoulder at where Evangeline sat somewhere behind us. I sensed her eyes on us.

"She seems like too much. I guess she is what you would consider too far?"

He nodded.

"Yes. She is way too much and way too far. And she's determined to hang a one-hundred million-dollar deal over my head if I don't agree to this engagement my parents cooked up."

I leaned over the table, fighting to keep my mouth from flying open.

"A hundred million dollars? You're kidding, right?"

He swallowed hard. "No, I'm not kidding. This deal could take our status from millionaire to billionaire, and my parents have hung that responsibility on my shoulders with the daughter of not only a board member but a contributing partner in our company."

"Damn, Atlas. How do you deal with all this: the ex-wife, the side job, your parents planning out your life, a want-to-be wife, and the stress of having to run the company for your family?"

I knew the Belair family was wealthy, but not that they were a transaction away from becoming billionaires. That wasn't something to take lightly when it concerned someone I was considering dating. More money, more problems wasn't just a saying. Sometimes, the people with the most money had the most complications.

And his parents sounded like real pieces of work. It was the cost of their son's happiness that they were using to accomplish their dreams. Did they not care how he felt, or was he another transaction on the road to their hopes and dreams? I could tell by the stress lines on his face that dealing with his family and their business was more stressful than I could have imagined.

"Without their influence, would you still try to accomplish the goal of upgrading your family's status?" I asked, sensing he went along with some of this to satisfy some of his own ambitions.

He nodded. "Despite their old-fashioned and often unethical ways of thinking, my parents did the best they could with me, given how they grew up. They were put together in the same manner in which they are attempting with Evangeline and me. My grandparents were also in a transactional marriage. Considering some of my friends' lives, trust me when I say, unethical or not, I got the better parents."

I couldn't help looking at him differently. He was rich, filthy rich, but he didn't act like the privileged rich that I'd come in contact with occasionally, and I was grateful for it.

"I've said this to you before, but you don't act like your status would suggest. If you hadn't mentioned it or if I hadn't visited your home, I never would have known how truly wealthy you and your family were. You're…"

"…Normal. Or shall I say, as close to normal as you can get in my situation," he finished for me.

"Yeah," I agreed. The knowledge made me appreciate him that much more.

"Now, I'm starting to see why you dance. It brings you down off that high horse you were born on."

He chuckled. "That's a good way to put it. It's something for me. A job not funded by my parents. A hobby not suggested by them. Friends I made that weren't shoved down my throat by them. Dancing has nothing to do with my family or family business."

"How long do you plan on dancing? Have you considered other alternatives to disconnecting from your family?" I questioned.

"I'm thirty, and in the dance world, I'm a grandfather. Most don't make it past twenty-six, let alone thirty. Therefore, I don't have many years left. The only reason I do well dancing is because, thankfully, I don't look my age."

My smile surfaced and spread slowly.

"When I first saw you dance, I assumed you were no older than twenty-five, so keep doing whatever it is that you're doing. However, when I saw you in a suit and tie for the first time, I saw you as a different, more distinguished man. I think the atmosphere dictates people's perception of you."

He grinned, and I saw him thinking, but he didn't reply.

"I need to use the restroom. Be right back," I told him, placing my napkin beside my plate. He stood as soon as I leaned forward to stand, showing me that gentlemanly side of him that I liked.

On my way, I didn't spot Evangeline or her cousin. *Good.* Maybe she had lost her appetite and decided to go home.

Despite this being one of the cleanest bathrooms I'd ever been in, I still felt the need to hover simply because it was public. As I was flushing, I heard the main door opening and closing and someone entering.

When I opened my stall and stepped out, it took everything in me not to roll my eyes. Evangeline was standing in front of the mirror, pretending to search for something inside her small clutch. She stood in the middle of the three sinks, not giving me a choice but to use the one next to her.

Lord, give me strength if this one says something to me.

I stepped up to the sink, briefly checking my light makeup, and washing my hands.

"Can I give you some advice?" she asked without glancing in my direction.

I lifted my gaze to her in the mirror. "No, you may not. I've managed these thirty years just fine without advice from random strangers," I replied. I cut the water off, shook off my hands, and picked up one of the neatly rolled towels.

"He doesn't date long-term, you know. A week, sometimes two, is as far as he'll go. He's just trying out different varieties before he gets married," she felt the need to say.

"I suppose I better enjoy these last few days before my time runs out, hah?"

My unbothered reaction to what she was telling me made her face tense in anger. A little vein in the center of her shiny forehead was throbbing. Did she feel threatened by me?

"If a man wants you, truly wants you, he will come to you willingly. You won't have to use money or side deals, and you damn sure won't have to hunt him down. Take a moment and think about the kind of life you're setting yourself up for. No love. No Trust. A man who screws you because it's his job, not his desire, driving him. A man who sees you as a stock option, not the woman he likes or even cares about. That is all you're going to have." I paused to let what I was telling her sink in. "Maybe that's all you want. Maybe you can only have what your money can buy because finding a man on your own would be too much like work."

Her head was cocked back, her body pulled tight and ready to blow.

"Who the fuck do you think you are talking to me that way? I could eat you up and spit you out without chipping a nail."

I shrugged. "If it makes you feel better. Do your fucking best. But, I'll still have what you'll never have, that hot ass sexy man out there chasing me because he wants to be with me."

She released a loud laugh. "You're a fool attempting to give me advice if you think he wants anything more than to fuck you. You're not on his level. You're not even a class lower then him. Not only will you not be accepted in his circles, but they are also circles that could eat you up and spit you out like the pathetic gold-digger you are, looking for a come-up."

I didn't wipe my hands on the towel but tossed it and shook the water off my hands at her. She was clearly baiting me into a fight. A deep breath did nothing to clear the image of my hands tightening around this woman's thin neck.

"You have yourself a good night," I said, walking off and letting my shoulder push hard against her to get her ass out of my way.

"Ouch! Oh my God, you assaulted me!" she yelled as two other women were walking into the bathroom. When I turned to glance back, they were scurrying over to her. She was doing a good job of holding her arm and had made tears spring up from out of nowhere. The two women, both older, glared at me like I was the devil.

"Did she rob you?" one asked, making me lift a brow at her, automatically assuming I had committed a crime.

"Are you okay? Do you want us to get security?"

Was I actually hearing what I thought I was hearing? While I attempted to process what was happening, Evangeline stood there glaring at me with a smirk in her eyes as she put on the performance of a lifetime for the women.

Those white-woman's-tears were a powerful weapon that had gotten many of us killed. However, mentioning such a thing to the closed-minded would make me the villain. Like now, me attempting to explain myself to the women aiding Evangeline would only make them hate me even more than their angry-eyed expressions suggested.

And to think, I was always labeled the angry black woman for speaking up for myself.

"No. Let her go. She's not worth the trouble," Evangeline finally replied to the women. However, the dare in her eyes clearly said she was willing to try all types of shit to keep me away from Atlas.

I underestimated the depths this woman was willing to go to marry a man who didn't want her. The bitch didn't know who she was fucking with. She had money, privilege, and a boatload of others on her side, but I had grit and determination.

I stepped away, acknowledging that another twisted drama was being added to the pile that was stacking up in a relationship that had barely even begun between Atlas and me.

Chapter Twenty-one

Dayton

Three days later.

"Okay. It's so good to hear that Trent's feeling better. Talk to you later. Love you," I said, hanging up with Callie.

I was parked outside the Oakwood Youth Recreation Center and sat in my car, watching the kids play basketball. The rim didn't have a net on it, but the goals on each end of the court stood tall and strong and provided a short respite for children—some of whom would go home to verbal or physical abuse and a myriad of other unspeakable dramas.

For the past seven years, my help in raising money and finding funding to keep the center going was one of my most meaningful side projects. This center had been the place where my brothers and I sought sanctuary after our mother died and our father was left to raise us.

Our father worked so much that the center and the lovely men and women, most volunteers, helped raise us. They knew us Oakwood kids so well that a few members had even acquired permission from our parents to spank us if we got out of hand at the center. I'd gotten the ruler across my butt countless times for stirring up trouble.

I stepped out of my car and approached the front door, waving at kids who acknowledged me.

"Hey, Ms. Davis." Demi and a few of her friends waved.

I waved back, flashing a friendly smile in their direction before they lost interest in me and put their gazes back on the basketball court and the teenage boys who were too old for their twelve and thirteen-year-old selves.

Entering the center, I inhaled the familiar aroma of food and the faint scent of cleaning products before heading toward the computer lab, where I knew my girl Toni would be hanging out. She was one of a few paid employees at the center who had volunteered here as a teen.

Homeless at eighteen with no place to go after she was released from foster care, the center became Toni's temporary shelter for three months until she could afford a place of her own. Although she'd worked a full-time job for years, she'd never stop dedicating her time to the center. After five years, she became one of the few who earned a paycheck.

Toni noticed me as soon as I stepped into the lab. She waved, but the million-dollar smile she usually flashed around like a magic wand didn't appear.

The eleven computers sitting atop four lines of foldable tables stood between us. There was a child at each computer with headphones on, eager to learn, and some completing homework assignments.

The droopy expression on Toni's face told me something was wrong. Her eyes held a tension that she was fighting not to show the kids. Her pasting on a fake smile when I stepped closer only added to my flaring stress level.

"Is everything okay?"

She shook her head. "Let's go to my office."

That didn't sound good. Were they threatening to shut down the center again? We had secured adequate funding to keep the place going for years to come.

Her office door was open, so she stepped in and flipped on the lights. Reluctantly, I followed her inside.

When she stood at the door, waited until after I'd entered, and closed it, the chaotic rhythm of my heart kicked up a few notches.

"I got a call yesterday informing me that a big chunk of the funding for this program was being stopped. They said that some bigshot business mogul was buying this place so they could turn it into a health food store."

"What? Who? Why?" I questioned, breathless from the blows the news had delivered to my chest.

"I don't know, but someone who works for the bigshot called me and talked to me personally after I got the notice that was delivered by hand. The woman I talked to said her boss was named Ms. Sutton. She even said you knew her and that you have the power to save the center from this buyout. That's why I called you yesterday to come and see me as soon as you could."

"What?" I said, my voice a whisper. "That fucking bitch," I muttered.

Evangeline was hitting below the belt with this one. How the hell did she even know I was associated with this center? What else did she know about me that she could use against me to acquire Atlas like he was a fucking business venture? Money meant power, I knew as much, but this was some shit I never expected.

"Do you know Ms. Sutton?" Toni asked, her face so tight with concern and stress, I expected her to burst into tears. "Can you get her to call off this buyout?"

I nodded, my mind overloaded with how best to handle this situation.

"Yes. I know her. And I will handle this. The center is not getting bought out and turned into a damn health food store. I'll make sure of it," I assured Toni, cupping her shoulder and staring into her hope-filled gaze.

She nodded, biting into her bottom lip. This center meant as much to her as it did me, and I'd be damned if I was letting some privileged asshole who used her money as a weapon destroy it.

***

I pulled into my driveway a little after four, opened my door, and climbed out on autopilot.

Alarming my car and walking up my driveway, I wasn't paying attention to anything other than the view of my front door growing closer as I walked and allowed my thoughts to consume me.

A shadow popped up beside me, and I turned quickly, ready to deck the shit out of the tall, thin white man. Fist balled, hand cocked, and ready to punch, he jumped back and threw up his hands in surrender.

"I'm a courier!" he shouted. "I have a package for you."

He reached with caution into the bag slung over his shoulder, eyeing me the whole time. I hadn't relaxed my defensive stance. He pulled out a yellow, legal-sized envelope and held it up.

"Are you Ms. Davis?"

I nodded, eyeing the envelope.

"You've been served," he stated, handing me the envelope.

"I've been what?" I asked, eyeballing the package but not taking it. The green certified sticker and my name typed out in bold black letters let me know the envelope was for me.

I snatched it from the man's hand, and he wasted no time turning and getting the hell out of my driveway.

After struggling to get my door open, I stepped inside, tossed my keys and purse on the coffee table, and fell onto my couch. I ripped the envelope open, and all that moved were my eyes.

"What the fuck?"

My eyes zoomed in close while my brain processed the black letters on the ivory pages. My heart rate kicked up a gear with each paragraph I read.

"You gotta be fucking kidding me?"

I picked up my phone and dialed, my breathing erratic, my nerves set ablaze, and my pulse jumping hard and fast.

"Hello. How was your day?"

Atlas's voice was filled with the kind of warmth that should have eased some of my tension. It didn't.

"Your self-proclaimed fiancée is on the prowl. She can't get you to bend to her will, so she's going to use me to make you conform."

"What? What are you talking about?" he asked, his tone heavy with concern.

"She's using her family's money and influence and has threatened to shut down the center I volunteer at, knowing it will hurt me to see those children suffer. I was also just served with papers. She's filed charges on me, saying I assaulted her in the bathroom that night we saw her at Peppercorn."

"What? Wait. Slow down. What?" he questioned, unsure of what to make of what I was saying.

"You need to handle this shit, or I will. I may not have a lot of money to back up my actions, but trust me, Atlas, your future wife doesn't want to fuck around and find out what type of vindictive bitch I can be when you make me an enemy."

"I'm so sorry, Dayton," he said. I could hear him rummaging around in the background. "I'm going to see her right now. I promise you, I'll put an end to this shit. I can't believe she would do something like this."

His jingling keys and harsh breathing sounded over the line.

"I'll call you as soon as I can," he promised.

"Okay," I replied before clicking off.

I liked Atlas. He was a good man with good intentions, but the drama surrounding his life was pure chaos. I could tell by the way he spoke that he'd been dealing with this shit his whole life. He'd learned to live and maneuver around it. Not me. I didn't have any intention of learning how to live with this type of drama.

Chapter Twenty-two

Atlas

Four hours later.

I sat outside Dayton's house, contemplating whether or not I should see her. It was my pursuit of her that had landed her in the type of drama that some of the people I knew thrived on. Everyone had their fair share of commotion encircling their lives, but the drama surrounding me was wielded by people with a lot of money and arrogance.

After pushing the door open, I stepped out of my car and took cautious steps up Dayton's driveway. The walk was torturous as I didn't have any good news to deliver. Her front door cracked open when I stepped into the little entryway. She stood in the doorway watching me, shoving the door open when I approached.

"Hello."

"Hi."

We spoke before I stepped in front of her, leaned in, and placed a soft kiss on her lips. Thankfully, she accepted.

I stepped inside and waited. She closed the door and stood facing it for a few lingering seconds before she turned to me. I reached for her hand, and she stared at mine for a moment before reaching out to receive it.

We walked to the couch together, allowing silence to fill the space until the words I wanted to say to ease her mind came to me.

"I've made some attempts to get this situation resolved quickly, but Evangeline has made herself unavailable, probably so that I won't be able to talk her out of this dramatic tantrum she's throwing."

The tension between Dayton's big, pretty eyes revealed her stress level. Her head dropped, and her chin lowered to her chest. She wasn't used to defeat. It was one of the first things I learned about her.

I pulled her into me, squeezing her into a tight caress. "I'll take care of this. I will not allow you to suffer because of me. It is a promise I will not break," I told her.

She glanced up at me then, shaking her head.

"This is not your fault, Atlas. None of this is your fault. If you want someone to blame, it needs to be your parents for initiating this non-consensual marriage proposal and Evangeline for using money and power to strike at me because I'm in the way of her getting what she wants."

Her words caused mine to stall in my throat. I was used to shouldering the blame, often for situations that weren't my fault. Dayton was the first person who wasn't allowing me to take the blame.

"I appreciate you for not blaming me, but it was my pursuit of you that's landed you in this trouble. And I promise you, I'll do everything in my power to ensure you're not hurt in any way."

She nodded. "I believe you. However, I'll say this once more before I put it to rest. This is not your fault. You're a grown man with the freedom to pursue whoever you want, and you shouldn't have to be blackmailed or persuaded by money and deals to make everyone around you happy, especially if what you're doing doesn't make you happy."

I swallowed hard.

"You're amazing. You know that?"

She smiled despite the stress still tightening her body. I pulled her into me, and she allowed herself to be folded into my caress.

"My lawyer is working some angles, and I have people constantly trying to get in contact with Evangeline through multiple avenues of communication."

"I appreciate it. But there is something you should know about me. If you can't get Evangeline to back off, I will."

The edgy tone of her words and the truth etched between every syllable let me know that she was speaking the truth. She may already have a plan in place. The day we'd officially met, I followed her to a motel where I'd become an active participant in a crime, though justified in reasoning. I wasn't altogether sure how she would make Evangeline back off by legal means, but I already knew that I would use every resource I possessed to keep her out of jail if it came to it.

She leaned her head against my chest, an unexpected move from her. I enjoyed the warm press of her body against mine as the rapid rhythm of my heart pulsed against her cheek. The erratic flow of my energy and my emotions toward her was telling on me.

I do believe I was already head over heels for this woman, and the threats against her because of her involvement with me were killing me. I needed to find Evangeline, though I wasn't altogether sure how I would convince her to back off from Dayton.

"You know what I could use right now?" she asked, pressing a sweet kiss to my cheek.

"No, but please tell me, and I'll make sure you get it."

Her hand trailed down my chest and didn't stop until it sat at the V between my thighs. My dick lifted like her hands held the magic touch.

"That can definitely be arranged. All you have to do is tell me how you want me."

"The way I feel right now. I want you to fuck me like our lives depend on it."

My brow lifted, and I turned, inching her back before I gripped each side of her top and ripped it open.

"Oh shit," she said, her eyes wide, her lips parted at my action. That one act set the sparks already popping between us on fire.

She yanked and pulled at my crisp button-up, causing a few buttons to fly and threads to rip while I pawed at her until I got her shirt the rest of the way off and unhooked her bra.

Lips smacked against hard and heavy kisses, tongues twirling around, wet and anxious, her hands working my dick one second and mine diving in and out of her open pants the next.

I shoved her back on the couch and jerked her out of her jeans, taking her panties halfway down her legs with them. The sight of her bare pussy with the little dark airstrip on it made me pause. Pretty, brown, and pink in the middle, her juices seeped, glistening against the light shining above us. I slung her pants carelessly to the side once I got them off and proceeded to drag her panties the rest of the way over her long, honey-hued legs.

Sexy wasn't a strong enough description for Dayton. She deserved to have a book of her own adjectives created. A spark of something potent, heavy, and charged possessed me—and her based on the way she locked gazes with me. We stared into each other's eyes, deep, searching, unblinking, and breathing like our lives were in jeopardy.

Her lips twitched into a smile, and mine followed right before we went back in, attacking each other with hard and soft squeezes. Her ass was in my hands one moment, her supple tits were palmed the next, and my fingers and tongue plucked her nipples a few seconds later. We weren't leaving out any parts.

Her strong grip worked up and down my throbbing dick, snatching my already rapid breaths. Attempting to get at her and work my pants the rest of the way down my legs wasn't working out well.

Reluctantly, I eased back, and she followed my lead long enough for me to rid myself of the final threads restricting my movement and her access to every part of me. Dayton's hand on me was gas-soaked fuel fanning a raging fire.

I repositioned us, laying her on her back with her ass resting on the tip of the couch. Her sexy, shapely legs spilled over the sides. Her inner thighs brushed the edges of the sides of my abdominals, making my skin tighten from the contact.

The view of her laid out before me at this angle put a whole new spin on the word hot. She was combustible, able to ignite my senses without trying.

I believe we had a thing with couches and sex. Our first time together started on my couch in my penthouse. Now, we were christening her couch.

The freedom of being naked with her warmth wrapping around me was intimate, sexy, and illuminating in the way that it made me appreciate every touch. Dayton drew me in so deeply I couldn't focus on one area because I wanted all of her simultaneously.

My hands ran along her shoulders and down her arms, her skin like clouds of silky heat. I teased a nipple, taking my time admiring her while she lay there, eyes heavy with lust, watching me explore her body.

I leaned in and sucked lightly on her left nipple before I kissed the tip, aware that I was leaning between her splayed legs, my bare skin rubbing against her wet pussy lips. She whimpered at my play, enjoying it, absorbing my languid movements.

My hands slid lower until my palms were at her silky thighs. I dragged my hands lower and flipped them to grip her inner thighs. The quick breaths and sexy pants she released fed my need to please her.

I lifted her legs so her bottom was hiked up and hovering over the couch. The position made her back arch while I spread her legs wide. I bypassed her dripping folds and licked my way down her chest and over her stomach, knowing it would produce more wet heat.

She hissed when the backside of my tongue licked over the patch of hair at the apex of her sex. The first taste of her when my tongue glided over her lips was like paradise. Due to all the drama in the past week, I hadn't eaten well, but I was about to rectify that issue and overindulge on her.

I lifted her higher to allow better access to her pussy. The move forced her to use her elbows to keep her balance since she wanted to watch.

"Atlas. Oh. Yes. Shit," she muttered, eyes wide and bouncing back and forth between me and the connection between her pussy and my tongue. I moved my tongue with a rotating thrust that forced me to control her hips.

Light strokes allowed me to savor her on my tongue before I eased the tip over her clit, circling it and then stiffening my tongue and sliding it deeper, tickling her walls.

She yelled out when I hit what was undoubtedly her sweet spot. I repeated the rotations with rapid loops that made her body shiver.

She sucked in quick sips of air and released them with keening hisses that were like siren calls to my throbbing dick. My tongue zeroed in on her pink clit peeking from the hood of her creamy flesh like a blossoming bud. I licked and circled, licked and circled, adding pressure with each rotation until she came apart in my hands, bucking against my face and cursing.

"Atlas. Fuck."

The word fuck was dragged out so long that I was worried she wouldn't take her next breath. She fell limp against the couch, her face aimed at the ceiling, and her chest rising and falling with deep breaths. She was a magnificent sight, her light honey complexion was purposely darkened to a golden brown, and the bikini outline around her tits gave you the true definition of her lighter skin tone. Although her tone was beautiful, I'd only ever seen her darker. How different would she look if she allowed her true complexion to shine through?

I prayed that she would one day embrace her natural beauty and not believe she had to darken herself to feel more comfortable around her own family. I could only sympathize with her on the matter because I'd never and would never experience the harsh societal pressures that stigmatized color and often weaponized it.

I climbed onto the couch with her, assisting her into another position, and my dick nudged her stomach as I kneeled before her. "Can my dick be the taste tester next? I can promise you, it's a much more thorough tester."

She reached up and pulled me into a kiss that melted me into a puddle. Succulently enticing, it drove me to near madness and amplified my desire to be inside her.

"Damn, I can almost get off on kissing you," I whispered against her lips while reaching down and lifting her so her legs were around my waist and the head of my dick was nudging her wet lips and sliding in with every passing second.

A lift, a few inches higher, and a hard thrust, and I was almost home. We both hissed and sucked in air at the tight penetration. She was throbbing wet and tight around my pulsing dick.

I eased back, no more than an inch, and thrust in farther this time. The action was repeated until she was shivering, and I was a push away from losing it too fast. I stopped, and she didn't ask why. She waited patiently, knowing that I would make up for having to stop so soon.

Deep breaths.

That's it.

I coached my way out of the danger zone in my head. The smirk on Dayton's face when I finally opened my eyes let me know she understood what I was going through.

Another cautious move back and a hard stroke into her made her lose the smile to an open-mouthed inhale. This move also confirmed that I had recovered from my moment of weakness and could proceed without caution.

The couch assisted me, allowing me to spread her legs as wide as I wanted while her spine was supported by the thick, wide expanse of the back. I worked her over, pounding into her hard and steady, her nails raking my shoulders and upper back.

Her body rose higher with every hard stroke until her spine was bent over the couch. Just when I was about to yank her back down, she let me know with volume and force that she was ready to proceed to the highest level.

"Atlas. You're hitting my spot. Whew, shit, you're about to make me...come."

I couldn't find the words to reply to her. They were just a mix of tumbling syllables swirling around my tongue.

"There. There. Oh, shit, yes. There."

My relentless pounding couldn't be stopped, turned off, or slowed down at this point. I fucked her, and she fucked me back, rolling her pelvis, meeting each hard downstroke. Her slick walls milked my dick for all it was worth. Our bodies were in a race, fighting to see who could devour who first.

We roared together. Gripped. Pulled. Clawed and scratched. We were hearing and seeing things that weren't there, calling out to gods, and grabbing things that didn't exist.

The hot, all-consuming sensations that ravaged my body and made a mess of me left me shaking, humming, and gripping her so tight I was afraid I would leave a bruise or two and my fingerprint would be tattooed on at least one of her thighs. She didn't mind, though, as her grips around my neck and her legs around my waist were as strong. We came together, an explosion of every sensation and some that were new and unknown.

My pounding heart was my only warning system, reminding me that I still existed and that I hadn't slipped into another universe. Next came the feeling of her still wrapped around me. Her legs loosened before her body slid down mine.

I backed off and allowed her to drop into a relaxed position on the couch. I rolled into a sitting position next to her, my head immediately falling back against the couch. Testing my legs right now would have been a mistake as I was pumped so full of Dayton's intoxicating drug. All I had the energy to do was sit there and stare at the ceiling, blinking and smiling.

"That was amazing," I whispered since my voice box was affected along with the rest of my body.

"So damn good," she replied, shaking her head, her gaze also aimed at the ceiling.

I could already feel the energy pooling in my belly, gearing up to reenergize me for round two. My stamina or desire or whatever it was had never been this ravenous. This was going to be a long night, and I prayed that one of us had the willpower to stop before we ended up straining or pulling something.

Chapter Twenty-three

Dayton

A glance down at my buzzing phone showed that it was my friend Priscilla calling. Aside from Atlas, Priscilla was one of my wealthiest friends.

"Hello," I answered on the second ring.

"Hi, Dayton," she replied, and I didn't miss the smile in her tone.

To this day, I didn't know who'd linked Priscilla to me. She called me to help her with the problem of her billionaire husband laying hands on her. Trouble had no boundaries. Rich, poor, black or white—if drama wanted you, it would find you.

Even though I helped her, Priscilla refused to divorce her husband. She believed she had taken enough of his shit over a ten-year span that she'd earned the right to live a pampered lifestyle for the rest of her life. She needed me to help her boost her confidence and devise a plan that would inspire him to revise their prenup and draw up one that would guarantee he never put his hands on her again.

It took us seven months for all the pieces to fall into place, but her billionaire husband folded like a piece of wet paper under the weight of the plan we enacted. We had put a whole new spin on the word *girl power*.

We had gathered pictures and video evidence of him not only abusing Priscilla but also caught him in the act of physically abusing a professional we had hired. The masses of information we gathered landed Priscilla a quarter-billion-dollar settlement in which she invested in multiple lucrative business ventures. She'd shown me how grateful she was for my help by dishing out a cool million. I used the money to help the youth center anonymously, set aside a sizable nest egg, and paid off my condo.

Over the years, Priscilla had connected me with more of her rich friends who found themselves in trouble with the monsters they married. The job of being a bulldog or fixer for wealthy women helped me finance the assistance I provided to women who couldn't afford to run. I had no problem accepting money from the rich and unfortunate to help the poor and unfortunate.

Now, Priscilla and her ten-year-old twin girls lived a fancy, free life in one of her husband's mansions without him. The best part of the deal was that he could never divorce her for fear that she would release the seven months of dirt she and I gathered on him. He would never be able to marry and torture another woman.

"Hey, Priscilla. How's it going?"

"Not good or bad with the ones you want information on," she paused. "If Ms. Sutton has any skeletons, she has an expert team guarding them like a group of Navy SEALs."

"Dammit," I muttered, hoping she could have used the resources she'd built over the past four years to help me find dirt on Evangeline to get her to back off with that assault accusation and her pursuit of the center.

"What about the other one?"

"Other than a few minor arrests when she was a teen and reports of her being a mean headache of a bitch, we can't, at this time, do anything about Atlas's ex forcing a child on him. There are a few things that can be done, but it looks like your guy has already got those bases covered. He has one of the best attorneys in this state on retainer, and I can guarantee you, she won't be able to sneeze without him knowing, let alone win sole custody of that baby. The firm probably already has enough to find her unfit."

I nodded, although Priscilla couldn't see me. It shouldn't have surprised me that Atlas knew people of that caliber. It did please me that he was handling his business with these crazy ass women in his life.

"This is the preliminary round. I'm just getting started. We'll talk soon," Priscilla stated.

"Okay. Thank you. I appreciate you doing this for me."

"You're welcome. Anytime you need me," she said before clicking off.

If Priscilla couldn't help me find a way to get these rich and wicked women under control, I could be looking at a serious charge all because those privileged bitches got their feelings hurt over a man who clearly doesn't want them.

What now?

***

Later that evening.

My buzzing phone drew my attention. I reached for it and paused at the word blinking on the screen.

Unknown.

I let it go to voicemail. They could talk to a recorded voice if they didn't want me to know their identity.

The phone buzzed again. I snatched it up.

"Hello," I answered, my voice filled with attitude.

"Hello, may I speak with Ms. Dayton Davis, please?"

At least they were polite.

"This is she."

"Ms. Davis, my name is Romando Alexander, Ms. Evangeline Sutton's personal assistant. She requested that I call you because she's extended you an invitation to attend a charity banquet. She would like for you and her to have a discussion in a setting that she believes would be comfortable for you both."

I pursed my lips. *Yeah right.* She was afraid I'd beat her ass if we met privately.

"I have nothing to discuss with Ms. Stick Figure Bitch. Oops. I mean, Ms. Sutton."

The phone gave off that barely discernible echo alluding to Evangeline listening on the other end so I couldn't help being petty.

"Please, Ms. Davis. It would behoove you to attend and have this discussion." He lowered his voice. "There's talk of buying the hospital in which you work."

"What the fuck is this pencil-necked bitch's problem with me?" I asked, knowing she heard me.

Now, she was threatening my job as a way of blackmailing me into a talk in which I already knew the script. This was a rich woman's attempt to get me to back off from what she wanted to possess. Silence filled my ears, and if not for the phone displaying the open line, I'd have thought he'd hung up the phone.

"Ms. Davis?" the assistant called, awaiting my answer.

"Okay. I'll meet her. When. Where?" I asked.

"Thank you, Ms. Davis. A courier should be at your door within ten minutes with the invite, which includes all the pertinent information. Have a nice..."

Click.

Now, more than ever, I needed Priscilla's help to find me a way around or through this shit. First, a flimsy assault charge, then the center, and now my job. This bitch needed to be stopped. This was why some rich people had so many problems and issues. They used blackmail and their money as weapons.

A few minutes after the courier delivered the invitation to the charity banquet, my phone buzzed again. Thankfully, it was Atlas.

"Evangeline wants to have a sit-down, and I agreed to go?" was how I answered the phone.

"You have to be kidding me. She's taking things too far," he replied. The tension in his tone spoke for his stress level.

"I think she was listening while her assistant spoke on the phone. I told him no, and he came back with, and I quote, "Please, Ms. Davis. It would behoove you to attend and have this discussion. There's talk of buying the hospital in which you work.""

A groan of frustration came over the line, and a bang sounded like Atlas had thrown something.

"This has gone too damn far," he muttered to himself. His angry utterance was accented with curse words. "I apologize for every threat, every harsh word, every inconvenience. It may not be today. It may not even be tomorrow, but I promise you, I'll deal with her. You're too important to me to allow them, Holly included, to think that they can get away with the type of privileged shit they are used to getting away with."

My brows quirked. He sounded like he was ready to trash the woman's house or something.

"If you don't mind me asking, what do you plan on doing?"

He released a fake chuckle.

"All I'm going to say is, if you take away the one thing that gives her power, she's worthless."

I wanted to know more but figured I'd let him do his thing. He already knew my stance on the situation.

"There is something else I'm dying to know," I said, needing to shift the vibe of our conversation.

"What's that?" He questioned.

"What are you wearing right now?"

The question made him chuckle, and I could already feel my mood improving when he replied, "Nothing, now."

Chapter Twenty-four

Dayton

A week of anticipating how this would go had me in a tailspin, and I couldn't break free of the swirling winds. Would I let my emotions lead me to a criminal charge? Would I end up in jail for snatching a bitch?

Would I get tossed out of this banquet because I couldn't control myself? The possibilities for disaster were endless. I had decided on all black for this event since it was bound to be someone's funeral if Evangeline decided to jump bad and test me.

A deep breath, eyes closed, and release. I claimed the calmness I needed to get me through this night. I would be rational and open-minded. I would do this without incident.

I kept repeating those mantras on a constant loop while my sling-back black stiletto pumps tapped out a beat to the rhythm of the words ringing out in my head. The smooth texture of my black, one-shoulder, draped silk dress kissed my skin, teasing along my curves, while the long flaring hem brushed the front of my legs and danced around my ankles.

"Thank you," I told the host, who guided me through the rose-covered archway that led into the banquet.

Smooth instrumentals, scaled down to the most optimal tone, played while the rich attendees laughed and bragged about their latest million-dollar purchase. Most only attended this type of charity event to make themselves feel good about helping the poor and unfortunate once a year.

I spotted Evangeline immediately after walking through the door. She was the eager one, waving me over like I was a missing part of her soul. I stood in place and breathed, letting calm wash over me.

When I didn't attempt to acknowledge her, she dropped her hand, chin, and that fake-ass smile. Embarrassment colored her cheeks when she noticed people staring in her direction.

"Your dress is exquisite," I complimented the first woman I saw, knowing it would spark a conversation and prolong Evangeline's wait time.

"Thank you. You look lovely as well. This is a Gloria St. John gown. I had it made last month specifically for this event," the woman eagerly replied.

As if I knew who the designer was, the woman kept going. I didn't know what else she was saying, but my smile, gracious head nods, and admiring eyes on her ugly dress spurred her to keep talking.

Living in this world had to be a curse. They fished for compliments, fake enthusiasm, and any type of attention. They didn't care if they had to pay, bribe, cheat, or blackmail for it. It must be exhausting. It was depressing to watch, let alone live through.

"It was so nice to meet you. My party is waiting and waving me over," I said through whatever the woman was saying. She was likely in her late fifties, but Botox, lip injections, and liposuction shaved off about ten years. It didn't matter that I'd just cut her off, as my next words would make it all better. "You and this dress," I kissed my fingers. "There is going to be a lot of envy in this room tonight."

The pride rolling off her could wipe out the city's power grid. I shot her one last admiring glance before finally walking away toward a sulking Evangeline, who was ignoring the ladies standing around her to stare in my direction. I was the center of her attention.

Good.

I was already ruining her mood. She stepped away from her group as I drew closer to her.

"Good evening. You look lovely," I said and managed to make the compliment sound like a real one. Whatever she was about to say died on her tongue at my unexpected praise.

One of her brows twitched while she stared at me, half-smiling and half-confused.

"Thank you. Our table is over there," she pointed out. "You look nice too," she said with a hard swallow like she found as much difficulty in being cordial to me as I did to her.

"Thank god," I muttered before swiping a drink from one of the servers carrying and offering up champagne and finger foods. Evangeline also swiped a glass.

I sipped when I wanted to gulp. My goal was to remain lucid enough to conduct myself like a lady.

"I'm glad you decided to come," she said, the air around us stiff and stale with animosity.

"I wasn't given much of a choice. My job and livelihood are being threatened because I'm going out with someone who asked me out. Imagine if someone fired you for dating a man who asked you out in the first place. The things people do in the name of fake love make no sense."

Contemplation played out in her subtle squints, frowns, and rapid eye movements. However, her distaste for my comments overrode her ability to choose common sense. I don't believe the idea of what she was doing was ever laid out in her brain with logic behind it.

"I didn't bring you here to argue. I wanted to…"

The announcer, who I hadn't noticed taking the stage, cut her off.

"Good evening, ladies and gentlemen. We have an exquisite evening of fine dining and entertainment planned for you," he stated.

I stopped listening after the first sentence and glanced around at the scene. The privileged and wealthy had paid a ten-thousand-dollar cover charge to donate to a worthy cause, colon cancer research. The problem was that I doubted they had one cancer survivor or current patient lined up to speak at this event. I doubted they ever visited a cancer ward or even cared about what the disease did to the victims.

All they were here to do was eat, drink, brag, and sling their money around like Evangeline. I was in a den surrounded by vipers who were way more deadly than the criminals who got locked up or carried weapons.

I bet most of them in this room had initiated some type of criminal activity to get what they wanted, all because they had the money to back up their claims and intentions. I would even venture to say that most of them had gained their wealth by the same immoral means. Would I be like them if I had money?

I shook my head at the idea.

"Hi, sorry I'm a little late," a familiar voice sounded, luring me from my thoughts.

My eyes bucked at the sight of Holly standing on the other side of Evangeline. She sent a teasing wave in my direction.

"Hi. It's good to see you with your clothes on, and legs closed this time," she had the nerve to say.

"It's good to see you enter this place legally," I replied, replacing my fake smile with a sour frown. Evangeline glanced back and forth between us, a million questions in her searching gaze.

"Let's go to our table...ladies," she finally said, walking off before we could spark up a good argument.

I strutted off, but not before catching a good look at Holly in her white silk gown. She wasn't a bad-looking woman. All she needed was a few years in an insane asylum.

Despite my distaste for her, I reminded myself that Holly was a woman, and no matter what I thought of her, she was at a disadvantage in this world, too. As much as I liked Atlas, I had to consider that I didn't know everything. I didn't know what drove her to cheat on him.

My gaze traveled in Evangeline's direction. Woman or not, there was no way I was giving her an ounce of leeway. She was a horrible person who would eat her young to get what she wanted.

We settled around a beautifully decorated table a few rows back from the stage. The chatter and music were cut off abruptly, and a tension-filled silence spilled into the space. The quiet surrounded our table before the weight of it pushed down on me. My sixth sense sensed trouble on the horizon. The couple who shared our table were thankfully in their own little bubble, laughing and talking.

"Why am I here, Evangeline? Or better yet, why is she here?"

"She has a name," Holly huffed, rolling her eyes.

"I brought you here to make a proposal. Holly is on board with it," Evangeline stated enthusiastically.

I already knew I wasn't going to like a damn thing that came out of this woman's mouth.

"Let's face the facts, Dayton. I can ruin your life with a few strokes of my pen. Instead of doing that, I can use that same pen to write you an offer. Write you out of Atlas's life for good. Name your price," she said, lifting a brow while she waited.

I leaned over the table and shot a squinting glare at Holly.

"Is that what you agreed to? A payoff. A surrogate is carrying you and his child. Did this female devil offer to buy the baby from you too?" I asked Holly.

"I agreed to co-parent with Atlas and stay out of his personal life. It would be difficult not to want him romantically, as I witnessed you finding out, but like she said, money talks, and no man is worth more than me living a nice, cushy life," Holly replied nonchalantly.

"I'm sure you received a lot of money from your divorce settlement. Yet, you're still greedy enough to fall for this bitch's money trap?" I asked her, leaning over Evangeline, who reared back in her chair to put distance between us.

"Mind how you sling your insults around," Evangeline warned. "I would love to enjoy making your life a living hell."

My scathing gaze met Evangeline's. "You have dirt on her, don't you? I've seen how thirsty that one is over Atlas." I was talking to Evangeline, while aiming my head in Holly's direction.

I scanned Evangeline with an up and down motion before allowing my gaze to reconnect hers. "Do you not have any self-respect? You want a man who's not interested in you? What makes you think that he's going to come willingly to you even if you manage to somehow get me out of the way?"

"He's a man. They don't know what the hell they want until you tell them."

This woman was more delusional than I assumed.

"That little help center in which you volunteer, I signed the final paperwork acquiring it today. I could make a call right now and have it shut down by tomorrow, and where are all those poor little hungry ghetto kids going to go?"

Even Holly flinched at those words.

Breathe, I told myself.

My eyes fell closed, and my fist clenched and unclenched at my sides.

"Monday, I have a meeting that will set me on the path to acquiring the hospital where you work."

"And I'll get another job," I said, opening my eyes. "Who do you think you are, running around threatening and ruining people's lives to get what you want? Have you considered the lives you'll be ruining in the process just so you can be laid up with a man who sees right through you? I don't get it. I don't get you."

"He and I are a lot more acquainted than you think," she said, lifting a brow when her threats weren't getting me to cave into her demands.

"I know. He told me he fucked you in his office. Bent you over his desk. He said he only fucked you to close a deal with your family. How fucked up is that when the man you want will only fuck you for money? That's sad."

Out of the corner of my eye, I saw Holly's brows lift high on her head. She was as quiet as a mouse, hearing shit she probably never thought she would hear.

Evangeline aimed a stiff, angry finger in my face.

"You..."

Shattering glass, loud and splintering, stopped all movement when a large portion of the room's centerpiece, a massive glass sculpture of a cancer ribbon, exploded. People ran and ducked for cover, some diving out of the way of the glass raining down and spilling onto some tables and skittering over the floor.

"What the hell?" I muttered.

Heart in my throat, I sat as slack-jawed as everyone else, especially when five masked men with machine guns fanned out over the room.

"Is this a part of the show or something?" I asked Evangeline while my eyes chased the men's movements. The program for this event didn't say shit about a live theater performance. "Are we being robbed? And if so, for what?" I asked.

"I don't know," Evangeline finally answered, the tremble in her tone making the scene much more real.

"What's going on?" Holly asked, her voice cracking while she placed a caring hand in front of her stomach like she was the one carrying her and Atlas's baby.

Chapter Twenty-five

Dayton

"If you haven't figured it out, we are here to rob you. That's right. We are here to collect from you rich shit-bags." The one speaking from the stage pointed a stiff finger into his chest. "I have nothing to lose, so if you test me…"

He lifted his gun and aimed it at what was left of the glass sculpture.

Tap!

Tap!

Tap!

More glass shattered, causing people to scream and cry out for their lives. I placed a hand over my heart to keep it from jumping out of my chest. These men were about to rob these people…us.

Holy shit!

One man from each side of the room flicked large black sacks open before going to the table nearest them to start collecting valuables.

"Give up the fucking goods or die for a piece of jewelry you can replace as easily as you breathe. It will be your fucking choice," one of the men told an older man before pressing his gun to the man's forehead for refusing to give up his expensive watch. The scene set off a round of gasps and frantic cries.

"Oh my god!" A woman sitting next to the man yelled when the bad guy slammed the butt of his gun down on the man's face after he collected the jewelry.

"The next one of you who gives me lip will have to invest in dentures, a new jaw, or a casket. When I tell you to do something, you fucking do it," the man barked and stared around at the fear-drenched, ducking, and cowering crowd.

Some people squatted on the floor behind their tables, and some leaned over the table and peeked up at the bad guys from behind their arms and hands.

What the hell was *I* going to give them of value? I wasn't wearing a mortgage on my arm or around my neck. My twelve-hundred-dollar bracelet and five-thousand-dollar ring were the most expensive pieces I owned.

The bad guy approached our table, and I dropped my eyes to the gun in his hands. Up close, it was even more terrifying, making my heart gallop in my chest.

"I don't have anything," Holly said, glancing up at the man with pity-filled eyes.

"Guys, do you hear this shit? This bitch who's wearing a pair of ten-thousand-dollar earrings just told me she doesn't have anything to give me," he yelled back to his gun-carrying friends.

He lifted the gun, threatening to hit her.

"Bitch, put the earrings in the bag, and for being a bratty asshole, take that dress off. It looks expensive."

"Please. Please," Holly begged. Why wasn't she taking off the fucking earrings already?

"I'm about to become a mother. You wouldn't hurt a woman expecting a child, would you?"

The man's head tilted to the side, not believing she was stupid enough to keep talking.

"Are you trying to tell me what my fucking morals should be? The fucking audacity. You don't look pregnant, and even if you are, you carrying around a future asshole doesn't mean shit to me. The way I see it, all you're doing is herding in another privileged asshole who'll do nothing but look down their nose at anyone with less money and social class than them."

He had a point. But I was hoping he didn't hit Holly with her stupid ass over there trying to talk her way into keeping something that her settlement and whatever Evangeline was offering her could easily replace.

The man's hand made a quick jerking motion at Holly's ear. Her shrill cry sounded off like something out of a horror film.

"I should blow your motherfucking head off," the man mouthed through gritted teeth. Holly held her bleeding ear, her hand trembling as she cried out, pleading for the man to spare her life.

Evangeline ducked lower, cowering behind Holly, willing to allow her to be sacrificed as long as she saved her own skin. The whole scene had my anger boiling.

"Sir," I called him and reached out with the few items I had for his bag. Evangeline followed suit, smart enough to give up her jewelry.

The man reached out the bag for us to drop our items, but he didn't move away from his position in front of Holly. He didn't even pay attention to what we dropped in the bag. He still wanted a piece of Holly.

"Now, the real fun begins," one of the bad guys, who must have been the leader, stood on the stage and announced.

He lifted a digital device resembling a tablet so everyone could see it. "It's time for us to do some money transfers."

Gasps sounded, faces expressed dismay, and heads sunk into shoulders. The announcement at least pulled the man's attention away from Holly.

These men planned to be here for a while if they intended to get money out of these people. Some of them held onto their money as tightly as a diamond compounded under pressure. Surely, this upscale hotel had some security in place that would alert the authorities as to what was taking place. I chanced a peek, lifting a bit to see the entrance. It wasn't barred or barricaded.

The two who had collected the bags of jewelry walked to the exit, cracked it open, and handed the bags of goods to someone. It was why they didn't fear being caught. There were more of them outside the door, keeping watch.

I scooted out of my chair, staying low and being careful not to make any sudden movements that would draw attention to us. Despite my wanting to knock some sense into Holly's head, I couldn't sit there and do nothing while she was bleeding.

She jumped when I placed a hand on her back.

"Let me see your ear," I whispered. Her raccoon eyes scanned me for a moment before she dropped her hand. I used one of the linens to wipe away the blood.

"He didn't split it all the way down, which is good," I told her before reaching into one of the glasses of ice water and scooping out some ice to place inside the napkin. I held the napkin up to her ear.

"It'll be okay. Next time, just give them whatever they want. You have a baby on the way. Don't you want to be there for them? Evangeline will give you more money, so don't worry about what they take tonight," I told her, and swore I saw a smile sparkle in her watery gaze.

Evangeline didn't see the amusement in my statement. She rolled her eyes at me before placing them back on the man on stage, who was still giving instructions on how he planned to extract millions of dollars through a series of bank transfers.

I noticed him periodically glancing at his watch, which meant that they were on a timeline.

There was terror in the wide eyes staring frantically at the man talking with the rifle strapped to the front of his chest. His hand was wrapped around the grip while his finger rested against the trigger. His other hand waved and pointed daringly at the crowd.

People ducked, gawked, and cried. Some shook with so much fear radiating off them I felt the invisible emotion across the room. Whimpers and prayers sounded along with other indiscernible cries that formed a chorus of dread-fueled sounds.

This time, a different guy than the last one showed up at our table. Since I had switched positions and was between Holly and Evangeline now, the man approached Evangeline first.

He sat the tablet on the table and put his insidious gaze on Evangeline.

"Do you know your banking information by heart, or do you need to call someone who can give it to you?" he asked.

The seriousness in his expression said she better not fuck with him.

"I-I need to call my assistant," Evangeline muttered. He pulled out what was likely a burner phone and handed it over to her, along with a pen and a pad.

"Call. Get the information. And..." he lifted a smaller handgun, a nine-millimeter, and pressed it to the side of her neck.

"Please. Please don't hurt me. I'll give you whatever you want," Evangeline begged, her body trembling so hard it shook the water in the glasses on the table, one threatening to tip over.

"Pull your fucking self together because if the person you call suspects anything, it will be the last words you ever speak," the man promised, his deadly gaze locked on Evangeline's fear-drenched and watery eyes.

She swallowed, and the metal pressed against her neck moved when her neck jumped. Both her hands remained lifted in front of her, shaking like she was in the midst of a winter storm.

"I understand," she managed to say, but her voice was still way too choppy.

"Pick up the phone. Get everything you need to make a successful money transfer and hang up," the man directed.

She nodded, making the gun move up and down. She reached, taking the phone in her shaky hand, swallowing and breathing hard to gather her wits.

She couldn't hold the phone steady enough to dial. I lifted my hand higher, drawing the man's attention before I pointed at the phone still shaking in Evangeline's hands. He nodded, catching my drift about helping her.

I reached out and took the phone from her hands. Now that I was closer to her, I was in the direct line of fire from that gun on the other side of her neck.

"Breathe. That's it. Steady your breaths," I told her. What's the number?"

"804-267-2663," she said, her words still choppy.

"You can do this, Evangeline. You have to," I told her while the first ring sounded. "Breathe," I said before placing the phone to her ear.

"Lori," she said, her voice shaking but not as badly as before. She cleared her throat and regrouped. "I need to make an emergency bank transfer. Will you give me the information I'll need?" I could hear the woman shuffling around on the other end of the line.

"No. No. I don't want you to do it. I want to do it myself. Send me the information," she told the person.

A long pause followed before Evangeline picked up the pen and began scribbling frantically on the pad.

"Thank you. That will be all," she told the woman.

I removed the phone from her ear and hung up. She followed the man's instructions. He must have been aware that some accounts had a maximum that couldn't be broken without triggering an alert. Evangeline had informed the man that hers was five hundred thousand. If they collected half that much from everyone in this group tonight, they would leave this place with at least twenty-five, thirty, and up to fifty million dollars.

Once the man was done with Evangeline, he moved on to the next table. It meant that they were taking from one person from each table, I believed to preserve their timeline.

Peeking from behind a table with my two worst enemies, I took in the scene, still not fully believing I was caught in this moment, being held hostage, stolen from, life threatened, and death swirling in the air. It didn't feel real. It couldn't be real. This was not my reality.

"Aww! Please don't hurt me. What are you doing?" A woman yelled out.

The pleading cries of the woman being dragged off pulled me out of the moment of convincing myself this wasn't real.

It *was* real. This was my current reality.

"Where are you taking my wife?"

The man stood in an attempt to be a hero and save his wife.

Whack!

The sound of the butt of one of the guns slamming into the man's face reverberated around the room and the hushed whimpers and pleading cries stopped, leaving an eerie silence hanging heavy in the air.

Based on the way the bad guy tossed the wife over his shoulder, kicking and screaming, and stormed out the door, more fuel had just been thrown on our blazing reality.

Chapter Twenty-six

Dayton

Where were they taking that woman? Was something more deviant than this robbery about to happen? The men were making the money transfers. What more could they want?

"Lord, don't let them rape that woman," I prayed, shaking my head.

This situation was no longer about money or privilege. I didn't care who it was. No one deserved to be degraded that way.

The man with the gun on stage paced but kept a vigilant watch on the crowd while his finger tapped against the trigger of his weapon. It was a silent reminder that he held the power in this room. To a bunch of people whose power resided in their checkbooks, I'm sure this level of helplessness was causing irreparable damage to their psyche. The three collecting bank transfers continued their jobs and had cleared half the tables.

"We have a few unwanted guests outside," the one on stage said into the microphone, playing the role of tonight's emcee. "As a show of how serious we are about our business..." he said, leaving the statement unfinished. He approached a small table off to the side of the stage that held awards and picked up a remote. The large monitor to the left of the stage popped on, drawing everyone's gazes.

"No. No. Please. No," the husband of the wife who'd been taken yelled when his wife, crying and pleading, came on the screen with a handgun aimed at the side of her head.

The look in the bad guy's eyes said more than her pleading words. They were endless pools of nothingness, and killing that woman wouldn't faze him one bit.

The man on stage lifted his wrist to his mouth, preparing to speak into it while aiming the remote at the television. The man on the screen holding the woman at gunpoint maintained a steady aim, waiting for the word. The volume indicator flashed across the bottom of the screen before the blinking square rode the narrow line across the screen.

We collectively held our breaths, shoulders tight, eyes and mouths hanging open, hands over rapidly expanding chests. Involuntarily, I shook my head.

Don't do it.

Don't do it.

Don't.

I didn't know this woman. She could have been the most important woman or the worst scum on the planet, but it didn't mean she needed to lose her life, especially not over money. I prayed. These men could leave with what they had so far. They didn't need to kill anyone.

Something about this situation ran deeper than I could understand. From the start, these men held a certain level of animosity against the rich and privileged.

"Do her."

I read the lips of the one on stage, his eyes on us, his mouth delivering a death order.

Bam!

Every person in the room jumped before a chorus of cries and pleads began. The volume and intensity of every word rang with desperation.

"Now that we've finally gotten your fucking attention. When we tell you rich uppity fucks to do something,

I suggest you do it, or you will be next," the demented emcee said, his voice traveling through me like the blade of a sharp knife after witnessing the woman's death.

What more could they get out of us? They had all of our valuables and were taking money that, if they were smart, couldn't be traced. How would they get out of this situation if there were cops outside?

"All the money we are taking tonight is being transferred to charitable organizations. Don't worry about trying to trace it because we have it all set on timers to be delivered to random organizations across the country, in different amounts, and at any given time. It took us doing something like this to get you privileged assholes to give up a little extra to help those who often did nothing wrong but be born into a society set up to make sure they failed."

He sounded like someone who had been pushed to his breaking point. Did his statement mean that they weren't keeping any of the money they were taking?

My head constantly swiveled, frantically trying to piece together what they were doing here and why. They had murdered someone as a show of dominance over this situation. A few more tables were cleared, and the money shipped to some electronic vault to later be distributed to a charity.

This must have been a group of activists, and if so, was it possible that they didn't want to or even care about getting out of this situation alive? If they were willing to die for a cause greater than themselves, it meant every person in this room could die right along with them.

"They're going to kill us if they have to, aren't they?" Evangeline questioned. Her eyes were filled with water as tears pooled in the corners and dripped down her cheeks.

"I can't die. I have to be here for my baby. This wasn't the right way to do it, but this baby is the best thing to ever happen to me," Holly stated, rubbing the back of her hand over her runny nose and still holding the wet linen to her ear.

Too bad it had to take our lives being in jeopardy for me to see that she cared about something other than money.

"We're not going to die. We're going to make it out of this," I told them with a confidence I didn't feel. They glanced at me with hope, like I was their source of strength. The cattiness and drama we'd entered the room with no longer existed.

We were now three women who wanted nothing more than to live to see another day. Holly took a tight grip of my hand, her sweaty palm shaking.

"He keeps staring at me," she said, her voice low and trembling. I followed her line of sight, and my eyes stopped on the one who had been ready to hit her earlier. He was staring at her like he had a personal vendetta out against her.

"Promise me, Dayton. Promise that if something happens to me, you'll take care of my baby. He's not here yet, but I love him with all I got."

Him.

They were having a little boy. Atlas had a son on the way.

"Promise me, Dayton. Please," she begged.

Her tone had dropped even lower. The energizing swirl of danger around us increased the longer the man stared at her, unblinking, his nostrils flaring. He didn't like the sight of Holly.

"You're going to be around to see that baby," I told her, squeezing her hand to drive home my shaky reassurance even as the man began walking in our direction.

"I don't want to die. God. Please. I'll stop with all the crazy crap I do to get under people's skin. I only do it because I've never meant anything meaningful to anyone, not my parents, my boyfriends, or my friends. I wasn't even my husband's priority. No one has ever truly loved me. This baby. I love him. Please don't take me now that I have this one good thing that could love me back. Please, God. Please," she begged.

Holly's prayer knifed me in the chest. Her pride had been stripped away, and she'd allowed her vulnerabilities to surface.

Evangeline gripped my other hand right before her head fell against my shoulder. She shook from the cries she fought to keep in, but they seeped out of her throat like they were being ripped from her vocal cords.

They were breaking down, accepting that they were about to die. I couldn't accept it. I wouldn't. I had to hold on to hope. We were going to make it out of this alive. These men were robbing from the rich and giving to the poor, so they had to have some kind of moral compass.

"We are going to make it. We are going to walk out of here stronger women," I told them, squeezing their hands.

"You!" the man who was now standing over us shouted. His crooked finger was aimed at Holly. "Get up!"

I shook my head. He wasn't that evil. He couldn't be. Holly shook with fear, so afraid, she was a crying mess.

"Please. I'll give you whatever you want. Please don't kill me. All I want is to see my baby being born," she leaned over until her head was bowed toward him. Her hands were in the prayer position as sobs mixed with her pleas sounded. I snatched my hand away from Evangeline, who had a death grip on it.

Cautiously, I moved, walking on my knees with my hands held up in surrender. I dragged my shaky body, heavy with tension, until I was kneeling beside Holly. I didn't know why he wanted her, but his expression had led her to believe she was not surviving the night.

It was still there in his gaze. The anger. The way his eyes narrowed and loomed over her. The disdain in his upturned lip. He wasn't the only one who carried that expression. The same expression of hate was duplicated on the faces of all the bad guys.

They hated these people simply because they were wealthy. Their view of the world couldn't have been that narrow. I'll admit that I sometimes lumped them all in the privileged pricks category, but I also had enough common sense to know that not all rich people were bad people.

"Please," I begged along with Holly. "She has a baby on the way." He kept glancing at Holly's flat stomach. He didn't have to know that Holly wasn't the one carrying the baby.

"The baby is innocent, untainted by this awful world. You must have some respect for innocent life," I said.

His face squinted into a tight knot, and I didn't know if it was anger or remorse. The door opened, drawing his attention before he could reply.

The one who shot the woman on the monitor re-entered the room. He drew everyone's attention as he approached the stage, and the emcee leaned over to allow him to whisper something to him.

When he aimed his finger in our direction, pointing at our table, I swore his aim gave off an energy pulse that pushed clean through my chest and ripped out my heart. My head shook slowly, left to right. They weren't about to do this. I refused to believe that they were about to kill one of us.

The man walked up, stood next to the one standing over us, and whispered something in his ear. Their hate-filled gazes raked over me, Evangeline, and Holly. To these men, we were their enemy, born of money and privilege, and they assumed we hated anyone who wasn't on our level.

The flaw in their thinking was me and others like me. I wasn't privileged or wealthy, yet tonight, I was being looked upon like everyone else in this room.

Mine and Holly's hands were gripped so tightly mine had gone numb.

Despite the fear riding me, hounding me, haunting me, I refused to let a tear slip. I stared the men in their eyes and faced their hate.

When the man doing the whispering, the murderer, straightened and moved, he brushed past Holly and me and snatched up Evangeline. She released a shrieking cry for help that spurred on the screams of others in the room.

"Dayton! Help! Please! You can't let them take me. Please help me!" she shouted, reaching out for my hand. I took her hand, our grip locking into place tight with a strength I didn't think the skinny woman possessed.

The man had a thick arm slung around the front of her neck, the other around her tiny waist. He dragged her off, her long legs kicking, her expensive sparkling silver dress dragging along the floor. Our grip was locked so tightly that I was being dragged off with her. Evangeline's gaping eyes were focused on me. I believe I was the only hope she saw at this point.

"Take them both since that one is eager to go with her," the one still standing over Holly barked, his smile wide with a sinister glow shadowing his body.

Holly walked on her knees after us, her mouth wide and eyes radiating enough fear that I swore I felt it coming off her.

My hand was snatched out of Evangeline's when the man picked her up like she was no more than a blow-up doll and tossed her lanky body across one shoulder. With his free hand, he gripped me by the shoulder and snatched up my hundred-seventy-pound body like I didn't weigh an ounce.

I didn't put up much of a fight as he marched us, me being tugged along and Evangeline kicking and screaming across his shoulder toward the great big unknown.

Lord, help us.

Chapter Twenty-seven

Dayton

The door opened from the outside, and two men waited out there. This hall was cordoned off for the banquet guests, so the door leading into the hotel was shut and locked to anyone wishing to enter this area.

Where were the police? It was just occurring to me that we were in the bowels of this building, somewhere along the side, so how could the police find us, let alone see us?

This was a five-star hotel. There must be a way to alert the authorities as to what was taking place inside this building. Why were these men roaming around like they didn't have a care in the world while the banquet hall was saturated with fear and crime?

The man marched us into a small conference room where another bad guy was in there with… I gasped. The woman they led us to believe they'd shot on screen was alive. She wasn't dead? They hadn't killed her? They had fooled us.

Was acting out her death their way of getting us to comply with their demands?

I was shocked but concerned—what were they planning to do with us now?

The man tossed Evangeline off his shoulder, and her bare feet slapped against the hardwood floor. Somewhere along our walk out of the banquet, she'd lost both her heels. She ran to me, slung her arms around my waist, and buried her face in my shoulder. It was funny that she'd wanted to ruin my life less than an hour ago, and now she hung on to me like I was the last drop of water in the desert.

Our world was crumbling around us now, but would she resume her stance of destroying me after we made it out of this situation?

The two men talked, and the woman they had used to scare the living hell out of us glanced at us through her puffy eyes, tears dropping over her cheeks.

The men continued to talk in a hushed tone so that we couldn't hear them.

"Keep them here and quiet. We have to wrap this shit up," the one who had so graciously ushered Evangeline and me in stated before marching off.

He slammed the door behind him, leaving us in the care of the other. This man wore glasses. He was older, distinguished with the air of a college professor.

"You ladies can have a seat," the man said, aiming his hand at the conference table. I moved, and Evangeline's grip around my waist tightened.

"It's okay. Let's sit," I said, moving to the side of the table farthest from the man and getting our backs away from the door.

The silence that followed loomed over us, filled the room, and threatened to suffocate me. Time ticked by like a teasing bully, each second adding to the weight of our uncertainty.

After what felt like an hour of tense silence, only broken by sniffs and whimpers, the man's unnerving ability to stand in place without moving was finally broken. He lifted his arm to glance at his watch. It must have been their way of communicating with each other.

"Ladies, I need you to place your heads on the desk and keep them down. You do that, and I promise you will go home tonight and celebrate life with drinks and a good story to tell your loved ones later.

Evangeline reached over and gripped my hand. I didn't know what it was in this specific man's eyes, but I believed him. I leaned over the table, aiming to lay my head down while nodding at Evangeline to do the same. The other woman already had her face down, with her head folded behind her forearms.

Since our hands were gripped tightly atop the table, Evangeline and I were left with one arm to support our heads. It also left my line of sight open to watch the man take silent steps toward the door. With each step he took, I prayed that he wouldn't change his mind and return.

He eased the door open and stepped through the opening without casting us a parting glance. When he pulled it closed behind him, I blew out a sigh of relief. Soon after, an elongated scrape sounded outside the door. Was he barricading us inside?

I stood to walk toward the door.

"Don't. He may still be out there," Evangeline said, her eyes wide and pleading. She hadn't released my hand. Her other hand sat over her heart as she breathed heavily with her eyes aimed at the closed door.

"I think they're gone. I don't believe the cops were ever involved," I said, glancing at the woman at the other end of the table.

"What did they tell you? Did you hear anything? What's your name?"

"I'm Susan. They said they would let me live if I pretended to die when a gun blast sounded. I assumed they were playing a cruel joke on me and that they'd shoot me anyway. They even made me practice a few times before they recorded the fake murder. They marched me to the back door and did the scene in front of the door. At first, I thought someone was out there, but that door faces an empty lot. After they were done, they brought me in here, and I've been here since," Susan said.

I took a few cautious steps until I reached the door and placed my ear against it.

Silence.

Since this was a windowless room, sound was all that hinted at what was happening. Evangeline stood and faced me but didn't move to join me. Susan stood on shaky legs before taking slow and easy steps in my direction. She, like Evangeline, had lost her shoes.

"I believe they're gone. They've gotten what they wanted and have left the building."

Neither woman rendered a reply. They didn't share my optimism.

"We have to get out of here. If the authorities show up, they won't know to look for us here."

The comment got their attention. The space was no bigger than an average-sized room, but it contained shelves of books and a large cabinet I assumed was filled with supplies.

"Let's find something to jimmy this door open," I said, stepping away and going to the cabinets at the back of the room. I sprang open one of the doors and found what I suspected: office supplies.

Susan and Evangeline joined me, rummaging through the other cabinets.

"Do you think this would work?" Susan lifted a black marble paperweight. It was a square and a bit smaller than a Rubik's cube.

I glanced at the weight in her hand and at the door. The lock wasn't a big sturdy deadbolt, but one of those hotel-types with a sturdy metal handle. I shook my head.

"See if you can find some tools or a long, sharp instrument. It's one of those locks that can be taken apart," I told them.

"Like this?" Evangeline asked, lifting the letter opener.

I nodded. "Exactly like that."

It took me ten minutes and a lot of prayer, but I managed to loosen the main screw holding the lock in place and jiggled the rest loose enough to turn them easily. After removing the metal covering of the lock, I ripped out the internal workings until I was able to push out most of the front of the lock mechanism from the inside outward.

Once we had the lock successfully taken apart, I gripped the knob and stopped. We stared at each other, hope radiating from all of us for the first time.

I dragged the door open, praying the whole time that this was over and I could go home and drink until I couldn't feel or think anymore.

The hall was ominous and silent. Nothing moved, as though the space had been frozen in time. I glanced in both directions when we stepped outside the room, not knowing which way to go. One way led us back to the hotel, but we would have to pass the banquet's double doors to reach it. The other direction took us to the back door that led to an empty and dark parking lot.

I took the first few steps toward the banquet hall, and my newest *best friend,* Evangeline, took one of my hands, and Susan gripped the other. The closer we stepped toward that banquet hall, the more I wanted to take off and run.

Swish!

The door to the banquet hall sprang open and stopped us in our tracks, our gasps sounding like one big gust of wind.

The sight of a police officer breathed new life into me, and I inhaled a deep, relieved breath. However, it was his brandished weapon that drew my attention. We stood in place, not knowing whether to be relieved or horrified.

"Is there anyone else besides you three out here?" he questioned and thankfully glanced past us for the bad guys. Another officer stepped out the door while the first approached us cautiously, his weapon aimed at the floor.

"They made me pretend to be dead," Susan spoke up, her wide, unblinking eyes on the officer's gun.

"Are you ladies alone?"

"Yes, officer, we're alone," I answered. "They locked us in that conference room back there."

I pointed him in the direction of the office with a head gesture since my hands were occupied on either side of me. The other officer went in the opposite direction of the conference room, his grip on his weapon tightening.

"We are going to need you to return to the banquet hall. We believe the suspects are still at large."

He didn't have to tell us twice. We zipped past the officer and entered the room, still packed with people, only this time, they were all seated behind tables. Multiple police officers walked about while one stood in front of the stage with a microphone in his hand.

"Susan. Oh my God. Susan!" her husband yelled and took off in our direction despite the officer near him yelling at him to stop. The couple fell into each other's arms, crying and laughing. The sight of their reunion made my smile surface.

The next thing I knew, Holly came barreling out of nowhere, tackling Evangeline and me.

"I'm glad to see you two. I thought those psychopaths were going to kill you."

"We're still in one piece," I replied, although I couldn't say the same for our mental state.

Were we BFF's now? The idea had me fighting back a chuckle. In a matter of hours, our lives had been flipped on its head, and the situation put into perspective that nothing was worth a damn if we weren't alive to enjoy it, achieve it, celebrate it, and to love, care, and be loved.

The next three hours went by in a blur. We were questioned extensively while the authorities took an inventory of what had been taken and what we remembered about the bad guys.

Now that it was over, and as hard as it might be for others to see it my way, I no longer thought the men were *all* bad. They had taken millions from people who could afford it and given it to people who needed it, some for the most basic necessities.

Should the guys who robbed this place be punished for committing a crime? I didn't know. No one had been hurt, although they had caused a lot of emotional trauma. My viewpoint was skewed because I wasn't above doing something criminal to help others, especially women.

"Thank you," Evangeline stated when we were finally released and walking out of the banquet back into the hotel. Holly had left ahead of us with the first leg of people who were released.

"For what?" I finally asked Evangeline.

"You put yourself at risk for Holly and me. I think it's safe to say a huge life lesson was learned here tonight," she pointed out.

I nodded, agreeing.

"I'm probably still going to be a mean bitch. It's in my nature. But the petty anger I harbored toward you no longer exists. The threats I tossed around no longer exist. I will back off and graciously accept that Atlas isn't mine, and I can't make him mine simply because I have the power to do it. I never had any intention of buying or selling the youth center or the hospital," she said, pausing before releasing a relieving chuckle. "I believe I needed to experience this traumatic event. My eyes needed to be opened. I needed to be shown that I can't control everything, and in the grand scheme of things, I don't have any control."

"Dayton!"

The sound of my name being shouted broke into Evangeline's moment of self-reflection.

"Atlas," I whispered at the sight of him, unconsciously moving closer to him. Forever passed in a few seconds, my smile growing wide and me moving fast enough for my fist to start pumping.

Atlas ran to me, his eyes wide with joy and relief. The moment he swept me up into his arms, I melted into him, folding myself around him.

"Dayton. Oh, God. I'm so glad you're okay. I don't know what I would do if something happened to you. I love you. I love you so much," he said into my hair and neck.

His words stunned me until a reel of tonight's events reminded me not to hold back on the good parts of life. I accepted that loving Atlas didn't take away from me but nourished me in a way that gave me a newfound respect for living.

"I love you, too," I replied, making him release a joy-filled chuckle and squeeze me tighter.

More people from the banquet hall passed us, smiling at our reunion, some nodding approvingly.

When Atlas did set me on my feet, his glazed-over eyes were cast with a new light.

"If I had the ring, I would propose to you right now," he said.

I didn't know how to respond. Thankfully, I didn't have to because I caught sight of Evangeline. Atlas glanced up to see her watching us, the smile on her face evidence that tonight had left an indelible imprint on her that she would never be able to fully explain to anyone.

"Are you okay?" Atlas asked her. The concern I saw flash in his gaze proved that he could look past the petty foolishness and drama she'd stirred up and show genuine care for her well-being. It spoke to his character, one I'd noticed from the start. I believe Evangeline understood that about him now. His concern for her was another lesson for her to bank.

She nodded and swallowed hard.

"I'm going to be okay," she replied, tears flashing in her gaze.

Atlas pointed between the three of us. "Are we okay?"

She nodded again, the movement making tears spill over one of her red cheeks. Her gaze locked with mine, and the admiration I saw radiating from her piercing eyes floored me.

"We're all going to be fine," she said before giving another small nod and walking away.

Epilogue

Dayton

Two weeks later.

I wasn't ready for Atlas to meet my father and brothers, but we had grown closer since the night of the banquet, and I was considering it. Instead of hiding our relationship from our friends, Atlas and I had told them that we were together, and we'd invited them to have dinner with us tonight.

"So, how does it feel to finally see justice served to that slithering snake of an ex of yours?" I asked Callie.

A twisted smile formed on her lips and danced in her eyes. Her ex, Donni, had drugged her multiple times during their relationship. However, the authorities hadn't taken Callie's case seriously when she reported him.

"It feels good," she finally replied. "He did everything he could to get off, but too many other women came forward."

"Ten others," Charlene pointed out. Ransome had his arm propped over the back of her chair, his hand caressing her back. He had it so bad for my friend, and it made me smile every time I saw them together.

"You could have told us you recorded Donni when you stole my car, snuck out of my house, and ran off to conduct your own little sting operation on him," I told her. I was still upset about her risking herself running off to confront him.

"I didn't want to say anything until I knew for sure that I had enough for it to matter. When I started reaching out to the women I knew he cheated on me with and dated in the past, their stories blew me away. He really didn't think that there was anything wrong with what he was do-ing," she said, her face squinted in disgust.

"I'm glad he got what he deserved and that his high-priced lawyers couldn't do a thing to keep him out of jail."

I glanced at Charlene.

"So," I dragged the word out. "Is what I heard about what happened to Carter in jail true?"

She pursed her lips, attempting to maintain her digni-fied nature without letting me drag her down to my level of pettiness. However, I spotted the smile in her eyes be-fore she nodded.

"Damn, he really did get raped in the ass?" I said, causing every eye at the table to cast a variety of expres-sions in my direction. I was only saying what was inside their heads, especially after all the shit Carter had pulled. And none of them couldn't tell me they weren't happy that Carter was getting his ass handed to him, literally.

The conversation died down after the food arrived, each couple falling into their little love huddles. Charlene and Ransome were tasting food off each other's plates, and Trent and Callie were nearly forehead to forehead, laughing at some joke he'd told her. I never believed I would enjoy seeing my girls in this light, but what did I know?

I jumped, placing a hand over my chest when one of the wait staff passed too close, brushing my arm. Atlas noticed, and he placed a delicate hand atop mine and leaned closer.

"Are you okay?" I nodded. He stared, attempting to gauge my state of mind.

"I know that you're tough. I've seen you in action. But, whenever you need to or want to talk," I'm here for you. He paused, his brows pinching and his eyes not hiding the concern in them. I flipped my hand and closed it around his.

"I promise you. I'm fine. The more I think about that night, the more I'm convinced those guys were activists who didn't want to hurt anyone. I believed they were willing to risk it all to help the less fortunate. I'm not saying that they were right, but if all that money, twenty-seven million dollars, went to charity like they claimed it would, then my heart rate spikes, nerves, and the anxiety is a small price to pay."

His unreadable gaze remained on me for a long, silent moment. My smile enticed his to show up.

"And I can't forget the fact that the night brought together three of the most unlikely people on the planet. I may be in jail if that night didn't happen. Do you realize that? It even gave you and Holly an opportunity to work out a plan for your son. That night taught me that you never truly know someone else's struggle, their pain, or the internal prisons they may lock themselves in until they are stripped bare and forced to show you who they truly are. I believe I got a peek at Holly and Evangeline that I would have never otherwise seen. That night gave the three of us a jolt of self-reflection we didn't even know we needed."

I chuckled. "Are we going to be best friends? Highly unlikely. Can we work together and be cordial with one another? Absolutely."

His lopsided grin met mine. The way I spoke of that night and about the women who wanted to wage war against me for his attention always enticed a smile that lit up his eyes.

My phone buzzed in my purse, calling my attention to at least see who was calling me. The sight of Priscilla's name widened my eyes.

"I need to take this," I told Atlas, standing. I lifted my phone to the rest of the table, who presented smiles before falling back into their affectionate huddles. Atlas nodded as I walked off and swiped my finger across the surface of my phone.

"I've been trying to contact you for two weeks now," I answered, not even giving Priscilla a chance to speak.

"Well, hello to you, too. I've been out of the country. Emergency with someone who needed my kind of help with a domestic violence situation."

"Oh," I replied. "I hope everything is okay."

"It's handled," she said, sounding like the character Olivia from the television show, *Scandal.*

"I heard about what happened to you at that banquet. And that the guys haven't been found yet."

I pursed my lips and squinted, scanning the long length of the hallway to make sure no one was listening, although they wouldn't have had a clue as to what my conversation was about.

"Did you pull it off? The banquet heist. Was that you?" I blurted out. It was a question I'd been wanting to know the answer to since it happened.

Priscilla laughed.

"As much as I would like to take credit for that one, I can't. Was I cooking up something to help you out? Yes. But the type of planning that went into that heist was extensive. The official investigation, that they will never release and that you are *not* about to hear me repeat, says that the suspects didn't even use bullets. Based on the way it was written, everything was rigged before the banquet started."

The information that I *didn't* just hear, hit hard and further proved that the bad guys weren't as bad as they wanted us to believe.

"I love you, Dayton, but I wouldn't have attempted something that elaborate and potentially dangerous to get two jealous women to back off."

Since she put it that way, it was crazy of me to think that the banquet heist was some elaborate quest on my behalf. It was also egotistical of me to even consider such a thing.

"You're right. It was crazy of me to even think it," I said.

"I called to make sure you were okay. Do you still need anything from me?"

I smiled. She was still worried about me.

"No. I'm okay, and the situation worked itself out in that banquet hall."

"Okay. I would imagine after that type of high-intensity situation that I would."

She paused. "I have an incoming call. Take care, and I'll talk to you later."

"You, too. Be careful. Talk soon," I said before hanging up and flipping my phone in my hand.

My thoughts traveled back to the night of the banquet. Evangeline was the one who had insisted I attend. She had also invited Holly. What had driven her to invite us to that specific event in the first place?

I needed to accept that the night of the banquet heist was a random event that occurred because it needed to happen, not only for the three of us but for every person in attendance that night. I believe we came out of that situation stronger, better people than when we entered those doors. I pray that a big dose of compassion was also dished out.

I moseyed back to the dinner table, where I approached Atlas, who glanced up at me with the brightest display of admiration in his eyes. You couldn't bribe, force, or blackmail anyone into looking at you the way he did me.

Instead of returning to my seat, I walked up behind him, bent over, and placed a tender kiss against his neck and jaw. I wasn't big on public displays of affection, but I was more grateful for things I would have previously taken for granted. I didn't miss the side eyes and twisted smiles my friends cast in our direction. Seeing me with a man was not something they were used to yet.

"What was that for?" he questioned, glancing up at me over his shoulder. My lips hovered near his ear.

"Because I appreciate you. I appreciate what you did for me. I know now it was you who set up that banquet heist."

He froze. His smile dropped, and his posture stiffened. He didn't reply, nor did he attempt to deny my speculation.

It was beginning to look like lovable Atlas was more like his parents than he was willing to admit to himself. A longer press of my lips to his cheek was followed up by a low whisper. "Thank you."

He kept his eyes pinned on me while I took my seat. There was a hint of guilt, shame, and maybe a little relief peeking out of his fixed gaze. The look alone told me all I needed to know.

A part of me was testing my theory. Atlas was the only other person I knew who had the means and the guts to pull off such an elaborate stunt.

He had just given me the final piece to a puzzle I had been trying to put together for two weeks, but the biggest hint hadn't occurred to me until tonight.

The day after the banquet incident, Atlas had asked me about my ring that was taken before I had given him all the details of what the bad guys had taken from us.

Atlas had promised me that he would take care of the drama that Holly and Evangeline were causing, and I believed him. I just hadn't seen a way for him to accomplish the vow. He'd also commented on several occasions about stripping the power of someone of Evangeline's caliber. However, I never in a million years would have considered that he'd go to such extremes. And he'd done it all while lingering silently in the background and letting his plan unfold.

My moral compass was a bit warped for thinking it and feeling the way I felt about him at that moment, but Atlas was my secretly twisted hero. A smirk rested on my lips, and a startling realization hit me like a ton of bricks— love drew me to him and held me in place, lingering until I got the full-range of Atlas's personality. Finally, after all these years, it had caught me, and I couldn't think of a better man to be in love with than Atlas Belair.

***End of Love Lingered ***

Blind Date with a Book

Don't feel like shopping around for your next read? Grab yourself a Blind Date with a Book.

All you have to do is head on over to (https://www.michelewesley.com/category/all-products) pick a genre and leave the rest to me, Author Keta Kendric.

If this is your first time reading my books, Blind Date with a Book, is a fun way of introducing yourself to more of my books. If you've already read my books, I appreciate you, and offer blind book dates by other best-selling authors.

Birthday, holiday, or just-because, Blind Dates with a Book are great gift ideas for yourself, your book friends, or loved ones. These hot Blind Dates arrive in the mail autographed and beautifully wrapped with swag.

Head on over to my Website Shop where you can use the coupon code HOTDATE15 to get 15% off on your order.

Note: Also offering autographed paperback books.

Author's Note

Readers, my sincere thank you for reading Love Lingered. Please leave a review or star rating letting me and others know what you thought of the book. If you enjoyed any of my other books, please pass them along to friends or anyone you think would enjoy them.

Other Titles by Keta Kendric

The Twisted Minds Series:

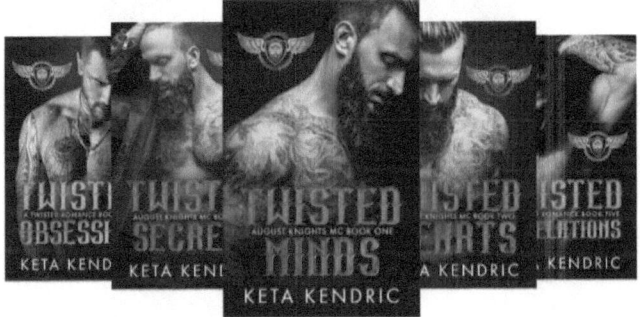

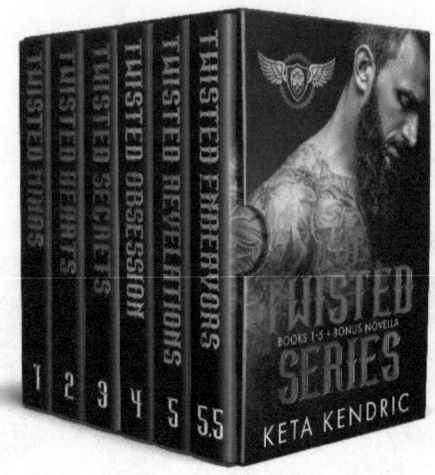

The Twisted Box Set

The Chaos Series:

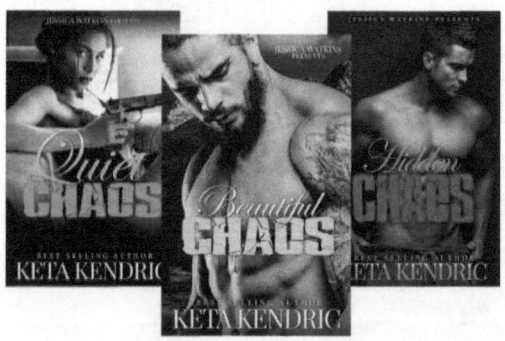

Beautiful Chaos #1
Quiet Chaos #2
Hidden Chaos#3

The Love Series

Love Lied #1
Love Whispered #2
Love Lingered #3

Stand Alones:

Severe

Roots of the Wicked

Primo DeLuca

Brizio DeLuca

Novellas:

Carolina Reaper

Mystery Meat

<u>Spice Cake</u>

Paranormals:

<u>Sevyn</u>

<u>Smoke</u>

The Box

Kindle Vella:

Love Lied Series

Audiobooks:

Connect on Social Media

Subscribe to my Newsletter or Paranormal Newsletter for exclusive updates on new releases, sneak peeks, and much more.

You can also follow me on:

Newsletter Sign up: https://mailchi.mp/c5ed185fd868/httpsmailchimp

Paranormal Newsletter Sign up: https://mailchi.mp/38b87cb6232d/keta-kendric-paranormal-newsletter

Instagram: https://instagram.com/ketakendric

Facebook Readers' Group: https://www.face-book.com/groups/380642765697205/

BookBub: https://www.bookbub.com/authors/keta-kendric

Twitter: https://twitter.com/AuthorKetaK

Goodreads: https://www.goodreads.com/user/show/73387641-keta-kendric

TikTok: https://www.tiktok.com/@ketakendric?

Pinterest: https://www.pinterest.com/authorslist/